Ellie's Great War

ELLIE'S GREAT WAR

A Novel of the Home Front

Diane Keech

SHE WRITES PRESS

Published in 2026 by
She Writes Press, an imprint of The Stable Book Group

32 Court Street, Suite 2109
Brooklyn, NY 11201
https://shewritespress.com
Library of Congress Control Number: 2025919162
ISBN: 979-8-89636-082-7
eISBN: 979-8-89636-083-4

Interior Designer: Kiran Spees

Printed in the United States

To

Ted

Anne

Mary Ann

Georgine Marrott

Thank you!

PART ONE

APRIL 1917

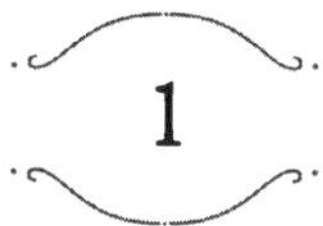

1

Aunt Ida's parlor door swung open even before Lucy and I reached the bottom step. "I knew you were on your way, girls," she said. "You sound like a stampede of horses clattering down those stairs!"

At least I'd made it to the bottom without crashing. I'd never worn a pair of high-heeled shoes before, so I hadn't noticed how slippery our front staircase could be. I'd have to practice walking in these shoes before tomorrow. Who wants to make a fool of herself on Easter Sunday?

Lucy and I had on our fancy shoes for the final fitting of the new Easter dresses that Ida had made for us. Well, my sister's was new, at least.

Mine was a hand-me-down that Ida had originally made for Lucy; I'd been admiring it for the past two years. It had been her first real grown-up dress, and now it was mine. Ida had altered it just enough to fit me perfectly. Then she had made it even lovelier by adding a gauzy, romantic white collar. *Diaphanous*, that's what it was! (I'd found that word in the dictionary a few days before, and ever since then, I'd been looking for a way to use it.) Ida had freshened up my old broad-brimmed straw hat, too, with streamers to match the dress. Those ribbons flowed down my back like the beautiful hair of a princess.

I couldn't help twirling in front of the mirror, not even caring that I was leaving myself wide open for Lucy to tease me about acting childish. But this time she didn't tease. Instead, she joined right in, and together we danced in circles around Ida's chair. Our fairy godmother, Ida, beamed and chuckled back at us.

A knock on the door interrupted us in the middle of our little celebration. It was Mom, just back from the last choir practice before tomorrow's Easter service. Her rehearsal had ended early. She had been preparing to sing a splendid Easter solo, "I Know That My Redeemer Liveth." When she'd practiced it at home, the beauty of the music and her fine, rich soprano voice had always brought me close to tears. She didn't just get the notes right, and beautifully right; she made you feel the love and hope and comfort of *knowing* you were safe in a warm embrace. Mom says that her skill at showing emotion in her singing comes from the opera training she had had years ago, before she married Pop. There's nobody in our church, nor in Foersterville, nor in all of Iroquois County, who comes close to her in bringing the music to life.

Mom settled down with the three of us for a few minutes. As she pulled up a chair next to Ida's, she seemed tired and sad, not buoyant as she usually is when she has been singing.

"Pastor Warner burst into the hall just as I was finishing my solo," she told us. "He was kind enough to say that it sounded pretty—"

Ida snorted. "Pretty! Is that the best he can do?" Then she looked at me. "Eleanor, you're the word collector in this family. How would you describe your mother's singing?"

I thought for a moment. "*Ambrosial!*"

Mom looked pleased at first but quickly got serious as she came to Pastor Warner's defense: "He had other things on his mind just then, Ida. He was there to make an announcement—a distressing one. America has officially joined the Allies in the Great War. We are at war with Germany. Pastor Warner wants to make tomorrow's service a more somber affair than any of us had anticipated."

"But Mom!" said Lucy. "Tomorrow is Easter! Easter is still Easter, isn't it?"

"You are right, dear. Easter is Easter, after all. But we'll need to tone down the celebration, the show. Like the service, it should reflect the seriousness of the current situation. It would be best for us to avoid bright clothing at tomorrow's service in honor of this momentous occasion."

As she reported this news, my first thought was, *War? What will that mean?*

My second: *What, no Easter finery?*

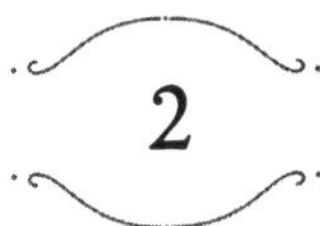

2

Just at dawn on Easter morning, I woke to a blast of wind blowing the rain (or was it sleet?) against our bedroom window. So much for pretty spring clothes, even if we hadn't had to dress like mourners because of the war.

Dark brown woolen dress. Heavy lisle stockings. Mackintosh coat. Galoshes. Winter. War.

Before breakfast, the weather lightened up enough for Pop to head out to the backyard on his annual Easter quest—collecting six blooming crocuses, one for each of us to wear to church. Those modest little flowers would provide the only bit of color on this gloomy day.

After breakfast, we headed to the service. Mom had gone early since she had to be ready to march in with the choir. The rest of us formed a little parade up Verona Street: Pop led the way with Ida on his arm, followed by Lucy and our brother Francis. I trailed along behind.

Church began with "Onward, Christian Soldiers," an odd way to open an Easter service. You'd expect to sing some kind of hallelujah hymn instead. But I love to sing anything, and sing it out loud and strong, so I supported those Christian soldiers with all my might. While we were singing, I noticed several members of the congregation looking quizzically around and whispering to each other, as if they hadn't yet heard the news.

The reason for the choice of hymn became obvious to everyone when Pastor Warner, who is usually a mild-mannered gentleman at the pulpit (if more than a little boring, in my opinion), rose to give a real stem-winder of a sermon that made us all sit up and listen. His words had everything to do with war and nothing to do with Easter.

"The time for turning the other cheek is over!" he told us. "America must administer an eye for an eye, a tooth for a tooth! The German Empire has repeatedly taken advantage of our peaceable nature! Slaying our citizens! Sinking our ships! At last, Congress has declared that such heinous acts must stop! At last, we are at war against the German Empire!" he said. "At last, America has added our might to that of the Allies in the cause of virtue. *Their* Great War is now *our* Great War. Hallelujah!"

He talked about the Great Sacrifice that our boys must, like Christ Himself, be willing to make on behalf of Right. (At last, he was mentioning Jesus, if only to make a point about war.)

War. I wondered what it would mean to be at war. I looked across the pew to Ida, who did know, I thought.

Ida had lost her fiancé, Pop's uncle Charles Foerster, during the Civil War—but not *in* it. Charles had been drafted as a Union soldier, but he didn't want to fight. Ida agreed with him. She gave him all the money she had saved as a teacher. That made it possible for him to pay a substitute to go instead. Just three weeks later, though, he took sick with the pox and died. Ida has lived with our family ever since. She is so cheery and active that you would never guess she had such a tragedy in her past.

Except at a time like this. I had never seen her look so old and sad.

Mr. Warner ended his sermon by announcing that a rally of all the local citizens would take place next week. The brave young men who were willing to step forward would have a chance to sign up then, he said. A caravan from the Foersterville Automobile Club would drive the group to the Albany recruiting station, where they would get their physical examinations—and their orders to report.

The service ended with the national anthem, another Easter first, in my experience. And Mom never did get to sing her beautiful solo.

Lucy and I raced home. A big Easter dinner was coming up that afternoon, and we had much to do to prepare for it. Ida stayed, waiting for Mom to change out of her choir robe. Pop and Francis joined the men of the congregation for a while to chat among themselves—about the day's big news, no doubt.

My first job before dinner was to set the big dining room table for eight—the six of us, plus Mom's brother John, who never missed a Sunday dinner at our house if he could help it, and his roomer, Reid Shoemaker, who had nowhere else to go for the holiday.

Like Mom before them, John and Reid had both moved down to Foersterville from Yankee Hill, where the farms are rocky and the roads are muddy. Anybody who wants an education beyond the eighth grade still has to board down here in the valley during the school year. Mom had graduated from the Foersterville school years before her younger brother. She had persuaded John to follow her down from Yankee Hill as soon as he was old enough to go to high school. He had lived with our family then; that's why I grew up thinking of him not as my uncle but as my much older brother.

Reid, on the other hand, is no relative of ours, according to Mom. (John disagrees. He says all the Yankee Hill folks are related—they just don't keep records of how it happened.) Reid was nineteen years old that Easter—almost twenty, I think—and was only just finishing his third year of high school. Lucy told me he was very smart, though given his age, I had trouble believing that.

While we womenfolk were busy with meal preparations, the men arrived and settled in the parlor for a conversation before dinner. A *preprandial* conversation, I'd say. (Now there's a good word!) From the dining room, I could hear their voices but not what they were talking about—even as the conversation grew louder and more animated. It was John who seemed to be doing most of the talking, full of exclamation points like Pastor Warner.

Soon Mom summoned everyone to dinner, and Ida and the menfolk took their places at the table. Mom, Lucy, and I brought forth the feast.

A whole ham was the centerpiece. Mom would have preferred a leg of lamb, her favorite meat, she says, but Pop has an aversion to lamb. She thinks it's because he's never eaten it rare, at its most delicious. But Pop hates the sight of blood on his plate, she says. She had served him lamb only once, early in their marriage. "Never again!" she would say. "Not after the fuss he raised."

I once asked how she manages having to stay away from some of her favorite foods in order to please Pop. "Thank goodness for restaurants!" she told me with a wink.

While Pop served the ham, Lucy and I passed out the side dishes: scalloped potatoes, soft rolls from the bakery up the street, Ida's special cranberry-apple-orange relish, fresh asparagus, carrots from last fall's harvest.

Then Pop said grace—quickly, so that dinner would not grow cold.

Only after we had settled into our dinner did I begin to make sense of what the men had been talking about in the parlor.

It was war. Of course.

Pop's dinner got cold while he kept making his argument. "This war was inevitable. Look at what they've done to goad us. Until recently,

I believed that the German Empire could never be our enemy—after all, Germany is the ancestral homeland of many Americans—including, of course, all the leading families here in Iroquois County."

"*Some* of them, not all," John interjected. He tends to get a little prickly when he thinks the valley dwellers are looking down on his Yankee Hill folks. "Being richer doesn't make you better," he likes to say.

"But the Germans have perpetrated acts of war—"

"So have we—like sending weapons and ammunition to their enemies," said John.

"Hush, John," Mom replied, seeming to sense an escalation that might soon get out of control. "*My* main concern is whether the government institutes a draft. What will become of Francis's dreams of going to Union College?"

Francis stifled a snort, or maybe just a cough, but said nothing. It made me begin to wonder if those dreams of Union College belonged more to Mom than to him.

"Money will not be a problem if it comes to that," Pop replied. "We can pay for a substitute if we have to, just like—forgive me, Ida . . ."

Ida nodded slightly, pursing her lips, but said nothing.

Lucy cast a worried look across the table at Reid. "You'd probably be eligible for a draft too. If it comes to that, could you or your family get the money to . . .?"

"Not bloody likely!" he replied, prompting a disapproving look from Mom. I'd seen her give that look to Francis, too, when he made comments she thought were vulgar.

I studied Reid from across the table. He didn't look a bit embarrassed about his faux pas. There was even a kind of wry look on his face, as if he enjoyed getting a rise out of us. Mom had been right. Reid was coarse.

Francis didn't say anything during this whole conversation, but his eyes were bright and he seemed to take in every word.

John clenched his lips so hard that they disappeared. That no-lips look is always a sure sign he's trying to keep himself from exploding. He didn't talk for the longest time. But when he did, I could hear the rage in his voice. "Draft or no draft, we've got no business butting into this European war!" he said. "We've picked a fight with the Germans by supporting the Allies with loads of money and war goods. What reasonable response did they have except to defend themselves against our own warmongering? Everyone would have been a lot better off if we'd minded our own business and let the Europeans handle their problems on their own."

"Watch what you say, John," said Ida quietly. "You could be looking for trouble. This is a time when your pacifism may soon start to be seen as treason."

A long, uncomfortable silence followed.

Mom broke it at last. Rising from the table, she said cheerily, "Well! It's time to get on with our own show! Who is ready for a slice of Ida's famous rhubarb pie?"

Everyone cheered and the party went on, almost as if nothing were out of the ordinary.

I was tired at the end of that long, turbulent day and went to bed early. I couldn't help holding my beautiful dress up in front of the mirror before I got into my nightgown. I guess it had been kind of childish for me to get so wrapped up in my own appearance when the world I had always known seemed to be coming to an end. I wondered if the dress would still fit me when the Great War was over and celebrating life in pretty colors would once again seem appropriate.

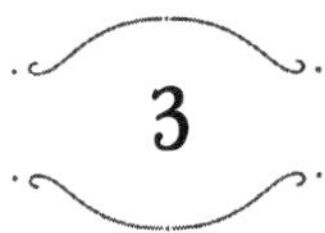

3

Lucy and I went back to school the next day. Another chilly, cloudy day it was, but late in the afternoon, the sun came out, if only for a few moments. I arrived at the kitchen door just in time to see the sunset cast a golden beam across the back porch and right across the kitchen. The sunlight fell on Ida as she stood by the stove preparing the family's supper. At that moment, she glowed as if she were lit from within. She made me think of the lithograph that hangs in the hallway of my best friend Rosie's house. The picture is of a saint—Saint Francis, I think. Birds have landed on his arms and shoulders, animals have gathered around his feet, and a beam of light glows down upon him. He looks awfully kind.

I gave Ida (my own saint) a hug, then started on my usual table-setting chore, this time at the kitchen table for the family supper.

"There's been some excitement since you went to school this morning," Ida told me. "Do you have any idea where your brother is?"

"Isn't he at the mill with Pop?"

"No. He left here this forenoon just after you girls went to school, but he never got to the mill. Nobody has seen him all day. Your father told your mother and me about it during midday dinner. He was irritated that Francis was playing hooky from work, but your mother was beside herself. She said that she couldn't help but think about Rags."

I'd heard the story of Rags so many times I knew it by heart. Rags was a dog, a special pet who always ran with Francis when he was a little boy. One day—long before I can remember—Francis and Rags were tagging along with Uncle John, who was looking for coal and other treasures down by the railroad tracks. A train came by. It hit Rags and killed him. John and Francis raced home to tell Ida and Mom, but since John was so much bigger, he got there well ahead. "He's dead! He's been hit by the train!" John hollered. As John told the story, Mother stood there on the porch with her mouth hanging open in horror. But then Francis cleared the corner, bawling but healthy, and Mom fainted dead away.

"Ida!" I cried out. "Are you afraid that this time *Francis* got—"

"My land, no," said Ida. "If the worst had happened, they would have found him by now. Three trains have come through here since morning, and no one has reported a thing. I believe now what I've believed all along. Something—who knows what—caught his fancy and he just followed it off. Remember, he's been doing that now and then ever since he was a little boy. I can't say as I blame him, though I must say it doesn't bode well for a life as a businessman."

"What you say reminds me of the incident with the invoices," I told her. Pop had nearly fired Francis for sending all of one month's bills to the wrong people. Francis had explained it as a simple error in alphabetizing the addressed envelopes as he prepared them for stuffing, but Pop wouldn't let him forget about it—at home, and I suspected at work as well. "I wonder if that mistake had anything to do with his disappearance today."

"It wouldn't surprise me," Ida replied. "Perhaps it was the incident itself, or perhaps Arthur's strong reaction to it. Or it could have been something else entirely. One never knows with Francis. I'm not certain that he knows himself."

It wasn't long before the family started to assemble for supper. Lucy was still exhilarated from her drama club rehearsal. Mom came in from her afternoon garden club meeting, and Pop arrived all pale and dusty with flour from the mill. The train went through as we sat down for supper. I looked at Mom as the whistle blew. She had tears in her eyes. Nobody said anything about Francis. I guess we were all waiting for someone else to bring him up.

We didn't have to. Five minutes later, we heard running footsteps on the stairs to the back porch. The door opened and slammed shut, and into the kitchen burst Francis, his cheeks rosy from exertion and the evening chill. Or maybe from joy. He looked downright beautiful at that moment, his face glowing with pride—like a young god or a hero.

"Guess where I've been!"

"Interesting you should bring that up," said Mom coolly, having recovered her composure upon seeing that her only son was safe. "We have been speculating on that very subject ever since you vanished this morning."

"Don't be sore, Mom. You'll be proud of me, I promise. I was walking across the bridge this morning on my way to the mill. I heard the Albany train coming down the valley toward the station. I asked myself—is it more important for me to be a clerk in Pop's flour mill or to show my patriotism by becoming a soldier?"

Gasps all around. Even Ida, who had predicted much of this, looked stunned.

"I wanted to get the jump on all those local boys who will be signing up at the end of the week. I wanted to be the first! So I took the train to Albany. I talked to the recruiter. I had a physical exam. I signed the papers, and I'll be leaving for training camp in Massachusetts at the end of the week. That's a little sooner than I'd had in mind, but why not go now? It's better than sitting around waiting to be drafted. I'd planned to come home on the 3:40 train, but I stopped to celebrate with a couple of other fellows who'd signed up with me."

"Celebrate? Drinking?" Mom looked aghast.

"Well, yes. But just a beer. Or two." He stood up erect like a soldier at attention. "And I am almost nineteen years old. And I am an army man."

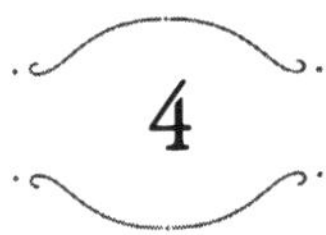

4

Even though John Sims is my uncle, I never call him that. I call him just plain John. He is a lot younger than Mom, closer in age to my brother Francis than to his own sister. John is thirty-one years old and still a bachelor. He is like a great big brother to me—the kind of brother you can take advice from.

John is the best photographer in town—and I don't say that just because we're related. He really is the best. He takes portrait photos, some of them hand colored like the ones of Mom and Pop above the parlor mantle. He also takes all the school pictures and just about all the wedding pictures—at least for couples who are married in our church. He also makes postal cards of local views and sells them at Mr. Lloyd's stationery shop up the street. John is quite famous around here.

He sometimes lets me help when he has a big job. He says I'm his best assistant because he believes I have talent. "You're a budding artist," he told me once. "You have an eye for composing photos and a careful hand for making them even better in the darkroom."

I think he flatters me—he's the one who showed me all the tricks I know. Still, I do puff up a little when he says such things.

"Believe me, Ellie. I've tried teaching all your predecessors too. But you're the one who has learned. You're the artist. Sometimes I think you'll be more of an artist than I am."

On Friday, April 13, John had his most important photography job ever. The recruiting rally that Pastor Warner told us about on Sunday had grown into an even bigger event during the week, beginning with a parade honoring Iroquois County's first recruit—my own brother, Francis. Pop told me afterward that it was the longest parade Foersterville had ever seen. Almost a thousand people took part—that's half the population of the village! Everybody else in town, it seemed—and plenty from the countryside as well—stood waving their flags along the parade route, which started at the high school playing field and continued all the way down to the depot, arriving a couple of hours before Francis's train was due. There the parade ended, and the speeches began.

For the parade itself, John and I set up our camera equipment on soapboxes and stepladders smack in the middle of Iroquois Avenue, just short of where everyone would turn left down Verona Street toward the train station. The marchers came toward us head-on, and we stood high enough to show a whole block's worth of them in one photo. Usually, John shoots parades from one of the apartments over Braun Brothers' Dry Goods. Those pictures come out okay, but sometimes you see more of the tops of people's heads than their faces. Shooting from the middle of the street was my idea. John liked it even though we nearly got knocked off our perch by the spirited team that pulled the firemen's pumper wagon.

As usual, Mayor and Mrs. Heinz led the parade in their bright red runabout all decked with bunting. He was so busy waving and smiling at all the voters that I was afraid he would forget he was driving and run right into John and me in the middle of the street. As it happened, he passed by a little too close, but not enough to graze our platform.

After the Heinzes came two automobiles full of old Civil War veterans in moth-eaten blue uniforms; some of the men looked to be nodding off even in the midst of the ruckus. They were followed by middle-aged veterans from the last war, the one with Spain. Some of them were marching, and others rode on horseback. They seemed quite prosperous, judging from the tight fit of their uniforms. Then came a ragtag fife and drum corps that hadn't practiced enough before the big event. Then a whole raft of school kids from first grade through the high school and teacher-training classes, all marching with their teachers. My best friend, Rosie Fairfax, gave me a smile and a nudge as she passed by with her ninth-grade classmates. After the students came the town fire brigade. The Woman's Christian Temperance Union all dressed in white frocks, the Daughters of the American Revolution in shades of staid gray with lace, the garden club, the Knights of Columbus, the Masons and the Eastern Star, the Epworth League, and bringing up the rear, the Automobile Club. Just about all the organizations in town were represented.

Mom, who belongs to nearly every club that admits women, would have had a hard time figuring out which group to march with if she hadn't had an even better choice. She and Pop rode in the place of honor, after the clubs and before the village band, in Doc Baker's cream-colored Franklin roadster. What luxury! Mom must have loved it. She and Pop sat in back, tucked under lap robes. Between them stood Francis himself in his new white woolen suit (a perfect match for the color of the car), grinning, waving, and tossing chocolates and kisses to the crowd, who threw flowers and kisses back at him. He looked like a dashing movie hero, and he seemed to love every minute of his fans' adulation. I was ever so proud of him.

As soon as the parade itself began to peter out, John and I gathered our gear and started down Verona to the depot so as not to miss the speeches. To tell the truth, it wasn't the speeches we wanted to catch, but *pictures* of them.

We passed our house on the way to the station. It was a surprise not to see Ida outside watching the parade. Whenever *anything* happens in town, you find her there on the porch, sitting in the big green rocking chair and doing her fancywork. Ida never misses a thing. What she doesn't see herself from the front porch, people come by and tell her about. Or else she just knows.

"Where's Ida?" I wondered aloud. "It's not like her to miss a parade. Should we check in on her, John? She might be sick."

"I'd say no. I believe Ida has her own reasons for not joining in."

I considered everything I knew about Ida. "She misses Uncle Charles? She's mad at Francis? Or worried that he might get hurt?"

John sighed. "Probably all true. But if I know Ida, there's more to it than that. Ida and I are a lot alike."

"*You* and Ida?" That's what people say about *me*. I kind of think of Ida as mine that way.

"I'd say so. If I didn't have to be here in all this patriotic whoop-de-do, I'd stay out of it too. I think it's stupid. Or worse."

"What's stupid?"

"These herds of people following your brother to the train station, waving flags, and making as if he's the bravest boy in the world. He has no idea what he's getting into. Neither do they—and yet they flock behind him as if he's the Pied Piper. I shouldn't say this to you." He cut himself short.

"I thought you were fond of Francis."

"I am. But he's acting like a damn fool, making a reckless decision out of nothing more than boredom. And Foersterville acts like he's a hero! It's bad for him, it's bad for our town, and it's bad for the whole country, this stupid Great War. You'll see."

"That doesn't sound patriotic to me."

"Most people would agree with you on that; it doesn't make them right. I'm sorry I said all this to you, Eleanor. You know that you and your family are very dear to me. It's the war that makes me mad."

"I understand," I lied.

"Do me a favor, El, and keep my comments to yourself for now. I don't want trouble over this."

"Sure, John." But I wasn't sure of anything—what he meant, what this had to do with Ida, what I thought of it. I put wondering away for the time being. We still had work to do.

I didn't pay much attention to what the speakers said, except to notice that each one seemed more long-winded than the last. We were busy taking pictures. We got a shot of the band playing "The Star-Spangled Banner" with the crowd singing along heartily, but we missed photographing the opening prayer by the Lutheran minister because we had to stand there with our eyes closed like everybody else. Anyway, it doesn't seem fair to take photos of folks with their eyes shut tight—on purpose, I mean.

Mayor Heinz gave a lofty address calling on us all to sacrifice as brave Francis Foerster was preparing to do. Some of the young men in the audience—especially the ones who had just signed up themselves—seemed to get pretty worked up as he spoke, but others, I must say, were paying more attention to Lucy, who looked to be flirting with the entire village band. Especially Reid Shoemaker, who sometimes fills in on cymbals. What she sees in him, I cannot fathom. He's short and broad-shouldered with black-black hair and eyes and pale-pale skin. He has a crooked smile, almost a sneer, and heavy brows that form angular peaks like housetops over his eyes. Downright Mephistophelian, I'd say, and Rosie agrees with me. I don't like it when he looks my way—he seems to peer right inside me and laugh at what he sees. Add to all that the fact that he's almost twenty, a little older than Francis, and he's in *Lucy's* class, two years behind where he ought to be. How could she make cow eyes at him like that? It embarrassed me.

Father O'Connor's benediction was interrupted by a train whistle up the valley and a great whoop from the crowd. All eyes popped open to see the high point of the whole event. John and I scrambled to get the best angle for the pictures. The troop train huffed into the station at last and slowed to a halt. Every girl in town blew Francis a kiss as he boarded the train, and they all pelted him with flowers too. All, that is, save Bess Welk, who seemed to understand Francis better than anyone else. She handed him a sandwich. We got pictures of all these events.

But wait a minute! My brother was leaving, maybe forever. In all the uproar, I'd forgotten to bid him goodbye. I ran up to the outside of the car as he was tucking his valise into the overhead rack. I reached toward his hand in the open window; our fingers just touched as the train started to move. "I love you!" I said.

"I love you too!" he called as the train pulled out of the station.

John and I got a few more shots, mostly of fellows as they signed up for the trip to the recruiting station. Then the crowd started to disperse, so we packed our gear and headed off to the studio.

I spent the rest of the day with John, developing the images and picking the best ones. I'd drop those off at the newspaper office on my way home. There wasn't much talk while we worked. I wasn't sure I wanted to talk with John just yet.

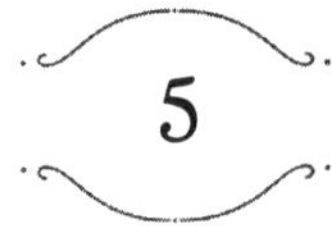

5

Lucy and I went to bed early that night. As we sat together in our room, each doing our hundred brushstrokes, Lucy kept sighing.

I opened my big mouth. “What?” was all I said, but it was enough.

“I think Reid likes me.”

“He may or he may not, but it’s clear to all of Iroquois County that you’re sweet on *him*! I wish you hadn’t made such a scene. It was embarrassing!”

“I didn’t make a scene. Did I? Well, he’s nice. And I was perfectly proper. Besides, he didn’t seem to mind.”

“I did.”

“Why are you so opposed to him? I think he’s handsome.”

“I think he looks like the guy who ties Mabel Normand to the railroad tracks.”

“And he’s very smart.”

“Why is he still in his third year of high school if he’s so very smart?”

“That’s not fair, Eleanor. His people are farmers who needed him to work. He couldn’t come down to start high school until just last year. And he’s aiming to make it all the way through four years of high school in just two. Sounds just like you! *He’s* read everything too.”

"Reading. That's all he ever does. That and get underfoot in John's darkroom. He's a drudge."

"That's what ambition does to people. He'll be the first in his family to graduate. And he gets no help from anybody. That's noble, I'd say."

"You're pretty far gone, aren't you? I still wonder why you're so interested in a diabolical bookworm—even a noble one."

"You're hopeless. Good night."

"Good night, Miss Normand. Enjoy the railroad tracks."

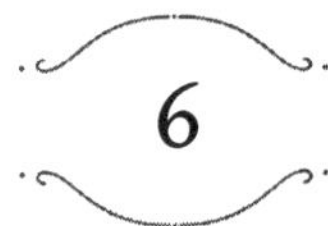

6

Wednesday's *Foersterville Journal* devoted the whole front section to a story and pictures about Francis's departure, the big parade, and all the other boys who signed up that day. There were lots of photographs, all John's and mine. I even got my name in the paper—under the portrait of Doc and Cora Baker singing along to "America," there was a tiny label that said "Eleanor Foerster for Sims Studio." I must say it's a nice photograph, and I *was* the one behind the camera. But John didn't have to give me that credit. After all, it was his camera and his film, and he helped me set up the shot. But John is naturally generous. That's one thing I like about him.

John got a good picture of me that day, the best I've ever seen since I was a baby. Maybe it's because I didn't know it was being taken. Most photos of me are ridiculous—I sit there with my eyes squeezed shut or my jaw dropped open, looking either demented, deformed, or deranged—or, on really bad days, all three. John says it's because I'm more at home behind the camera than in front of it.

Unlike me, Lucy always looks utterly charming in her photos with her head tilted just so, her curly hair a bit tousled—just this side of perfect, and the prettier for that imperfection—her Mary Pickford eyes just a little flirty and bold—though well within the bounds of propriety, as Mom would say. Whenever I look at pictures of Lucy, it's no wonder to me that all the boys seem to want to bask in her gaze.

But back to the picture of *me*. My picture shows me in my beautiful Easter hat with the streamers down the back. I'm in profile, or even a little beyond, reaching toward the train window. The window is almost like a picture frame; inside it is Francis, who's reaching toward me. I think the shot was taken just as I told him I loved him. The look on my face is almost like . . . longing, I'd say. I don't look pretty, exactly, but I do look interesting, like someone you'd want to know. That picture wasn't published in the paper, but John let me have a big print of it. It'll hang by my bed until my brother comes home.

On Monday came Francis's first letter. Pop read it aloud at the dinner table and then passed it around for everyone to see.

Dear Folks,

Here I am at camp after a long, long train ride with two changes and long waits in between. I was lucky to sit next to a real nice fellow, a college man from down by Cooperstown. He happened to be heading off to the same camp as me. Will Fox is his name. He had a cribbage board and a deck of cards with him and taught me how to play—no, Mother, not for money! You brought me up not to gamble. Well, you brought me up not to play cards either, but somehow it didn't seem to matter on the train. I forgot. Anyway, we must have played 150 hands on the trip, and I got to be pretty good.

It was about two a.m. when we finally arrived at the camp. We had just barely got bedded down in our new diggins when the sergeant came to roust us out. It was all OK, though. I was too riled up to sleep much anyhow. I sleep all I can now since they've got us marching and drilling from before dawn to well after dark. It makes a fellow hungry. I eat everything

I see, even though the food's not as good as at home and it comes on metal dishes, so it's stone-cold by the time you sit down to eat it.

Will and I have been chumming around together in the little free time we have. He's real nice. I hope you get to meet him someday.

Thanks for your letters and the pictures from the newspaper.

Your son, Francis

PS—Eleanor, you'll laugh to find out that Will mistook you for my sweetheart when he saw us say goodbye. He asked who that handsome girl was and seemed surprised when I told him you were my little sister!

Let me tell you, I took some ragging at the table after that. I myself don't see what is so funny about a girl like me with a beau—not my *brother*, of course, but some other young man. Some fine, discerning young man who thinks me handsome, and intelligent, and fascinating. Somebody who sees I'm worth knowing.

In the afternoon, I slipped off to scrutinize the new picture over my bed. Back in the shadows, beyond Francis, is another face, one I hadn't noticed before. It's a triangular face, or maybe heart-shaped, with a broad brow and rather finely made chin. He's looking in my direction—toward me in the picture, I mean—and he's wearing a big, easy smile.

He thinks I'm a handsome girl.

PART TWO
HOME

7

It seemed that everything around Foersterville had changed in the few weeks since the war began. The whole village—and the whole family (except for Ida and John, I guess)—was getting involved in the war effort.

John and Reid Shoemaker had been working secretly on a "wartime" project of their own. John made me promise to keep it under my hat. The government would soon start drafting young men of Reid's age, just as it had during the Civil War—except that this time, a fellow wouldn't be able to get out of it by paying someone to take his place. According to John, Reid wanted to stay out of the army in the worst way, since his greatest ambition was to become the first in his family to graduate from high school—and even, if he worked hard enough, to graduate from college. He believed that a few years of military service would end his education for good, given how old he was already. If he didn't graduate, he'd be back on Yankee Hill scraping the thin dirt like his parents and grandparents before him. And like John and Mom's people, too, for that matter. That's evidently what Reid had told John, and John, for his own reasons, agreed to help him avoid the draft.

The plan was for Reid to find a job that was classified as essential to the war effort but wouldn't slow down his studies. In Iroquois County, the obvious essential job was dairy farming. But Reid wanted to stay away from cows; they're expensive to buy, and they take too much time to manage—every day, spring, summer, fall, and winter. But *vegetables*, being seasonal, were quite another matter. Vegetables for the local market. That was the ticket, he'd decided.

As it happens, there is an island about three acres in size, Muller's Island, right in the middle of the Iroquois River, about a mile upstream from our house. It belongs to the Muller family on the far side. Because it is in the very center of the floodplain, it has the best cropland in the entire county. They say the topsoil there is over twenty-four feet thick. The trouble is, it's hard to get to. Bill Muller doesn't like to endanger his team by taking the horses across the railroad tracks, and the horses don't like the ford at the western end of the island. So, despite the rich land, Mr. Muller hasn't cultivated it for over twenty years. All he can do is to mow it once or twice every summer to keep the woods from growing in again.

I had been to Muller's Island many times. It used to be one of our family's favorite spots for a summer outing when I was younger. We had a big rowboat then, with two sets of oarlocks, not the flimsy little pram we use now. Pop and John, rowing together, would take Mom and Ida first to set up our picnic luncheon. Then they'd row back to pick up Lucy and me. I have fond memories of that place. It felt like a magical world.

I suppose it didn't seem so magical to Reid, who undertook to rent the island and set it up as a small truck farm with a few chickens on the side. According to John, Reid gathered up his books and his poultry and a batch of seedlings that he'd already started and moved into a little shed out there around the first of May, just in time to prepare for planting.

Everybody in town, of course, knew that Reid was taking up farming out on the island. What they *didn't* know was that the whole enterprise had been John's idea, set up as a way to avoid the draft that wasn't too obvious. They also didn't know that John had put up the money for it because he didn't believe in the war. That's what John didn't want me to tell anyone. I'm proud he knows that he can trust me to keep his secret to myself.

Back at our house, the telephone had been ringing off the wall since the end of April. All of the calls were for Mom. She and a group of other ladies—and some businessmen too—had been putting together the Iroquois County chapter of the Red Cross, and it had kept her busy. At first, she was disappointed not to be a chapter officer like Isabel Heinz, the mayor's wife and the only female member of the board. But then Mom settled into her role as head of the Military Relief Department, the group that would make supplies for soldiers and hospitals. The Military Relief Department was by far the biggest part of the chapter; though Mom was too polite to say so, I could tell she was proud of her position and saw it as much more important than Mrs. Heinz's job of taking notes at meetings and writing up the minutes afterward.

Mom is a dynamo of an organizer. I know a lot about her work because she hollers into the telephone, never having come to trust that her message will get through those little wires. You know how some people yell at foreigners in the hope that they'll understand better? Mom is like that—she regards the telephone as a foreigner in the downstairs hall. Pop tells her that most of the people she talks to could hear her just fine all the way across town, even without the telephone connection. I can't help but pick up her end of the conversation from my room upstairs, even with the door closed.

The first thing Mom did in her new position was to track down all the sewing machines in Iroquois County. She found the biggest group of them at the shirtwaist factory right here in town. She tried to get Ben Dowd, the owner, to give the seamstresses a half hour off work each day, with pay, so they could make up Red Cross projects for the soldiers and their hospitals—sheets, towels, pillowcases, handkerchiefs, that sort of thing. He refused to do that, but he did offer to let the workers use his sewing machines for an extra thirty minutes each day—*without* pay—if they chose to give up their lunch periods to the project. Mom thought that was the best bargain she'd be able to make, so she proceeded to persuade every worker in the factory to participate, and within a week, the team was turning out four and five dozen pieces a day. Mr. Dowd jested to Mom that his girls had never worked so hard for *him* as they did for her. She just stood up tall and told him in her chilliest voice, "They are patriotic *women*, sir. They work not for me but for their *country*."

I suppose I shouldn't have told John about this exchange. It got him going about the evils of the capitalist system and how those seamstresses needed a little less patriotism and a little more awareness of their own interests. "That's one thing," he said, "that they could learn from Ben Dowd. He sees nothing *but* his own interests." What they should do, he told me, was to organize a union.

John's socialist ideas aren't too popular around our house, but I think they're kind of interesting. I like the way his eyes light up when he starts to talk about greedy capitalist exploiters like Dowd and, well, Pop. Though I do find it hard to agree with him about Pop.

Like John, Aunt Ida doesn't believe in the war, and that is why she refused to engage herself in Mom's hospital project for the soldiers. Instead, she and some of the other older ladies who shared her needlework skills started a project of their own for Belgian Relief. They began spending their afternoons in our front parlor with skeins of pink and blue and yellow woolen yarn, making little layettes for babies in occupied Belgium. These ladies were whizzes at knitting, and some of them did crochet and embroidery too. They always took great care with their work, and their little sweaters and caps and blankets seemed just as delicate as if the ladies had made them for their own great-grandchildren. From layettes, they planned to move on to mittens and scarves for the older refugee children. But Ida refused to make anything for soldiers, even the sick or wounded ones. That, she said, was where she drew the line.

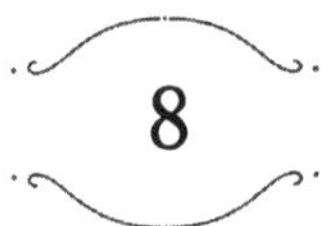

8

Mom and Ida were not the only ones who'd been busy on the home front. Lucy and I were turning into teachers! We signed up to work for the Junior Red Cross thinking we'd be pulled in to support one of the many projects that were already underway. Instead, they asked us to lead a whole new one, helping some fourth graders learn to knit afghans for the soldiers.

Obviously, most of these children didn't know how to knit, so we had to teach them, just as Ida had taught us. Ida is a great believer in using the carrot instead of the stick. She gave us the idea to give out ribbon badges as awards for performance—first finished square, most perfect square, largest number of squares, and so on. Ida told us that we needed to keep inventing new award categories along the way so that every child would have at least one ribbon to take home by the end of the project.

Although Ida didn't want to participate directly in anything that supported the war effort, she was willing to help Lucy and me with our own work. Even if that included keeping soldiers warm. I was glad Ida had shown us some of her old teaching tricks. I felt as though I'd been admitted to a secret club.

Once we began to collect the squares, Lucy and I had a whole new challenge—putting them together into bedcovers. The squares from all these new young knitters were of very different sizes and were even different shapes. We spent many hours trying to block them to one standard size and arrange them in a way that didn't look too misshapen; it took even more hours to crochet them together so that the blankets came out roughly rectangular. To be sure, not one of them was anywhere close to perfect. But I took pride in helping to create a beauty that was beyond perfection. I recognized that each soldier would see in his own blanket the evidence that all these children had done their best to bring him comfort in the cold.

On the day that Lucy and I finished our first blanket we got a short note from Francis. Pop read it to all of us at supper:

Dear Folks at Home,

You wouldn't recognize me if you saw me today. I've gained five pounds from hard work and good food. I am getting stronger and stronger. One day soon I hope to show the Hun a thing or two, if we only get a chance to get at them. I sure hope we see the Other Side soon, for I would not like to join the service just to wear a uniform and spend a lot of time marching around and shooting guns at targets out here in Massachusetts. I want to do my bit on the front where it will count, and I don't doubt that I will get back all right when we win.

Will Fox says he'd rather treat wounded soldiers than fight the enemy. To each his own, I guess. I like him anyway. I bet you would too.

Please keep writing to me—and see if you can get my pals in Foersterville to write too. Mail call is the best part of the day, even better than meal call. Bess may have lost my address. Can you give it to her?

Your loving son, Francis

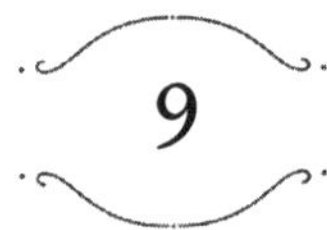

9

We didn't meet Cora Baker until three years ago when she married Doc and set up housekeeping with him just down Verona Street from us. Since then we've come to know her like family. It seems that nearly every week, we hear the unmistakable jingle of the buckles on her shoes as she trots up the stairs to our kitchen door. I love that sound. It bodes the arrival of sunshine.

These days, though, Cora moves a little more slowly, and she has to walk around to the front door when she visits. That's because she just became a mother. She brings little Vivian along with her in a baby carriage. Vivian is a wee, dainty being, the smallest, newest baby I've ever seen. I'm almost afraid to hold her because she seems like such a fragile little thing, though Cora tells me she's quite robust despite her appearance. Vivian is bald but for a wisp of pale hair. I wonder if she'll ever grow a glorious mane like her mother's; Cora's exuberant curls spring forth and form a red-gold halo around her head no matter how hard she tries to confine them in a proper chignon. "I do get to looking a lot like Louis XIV," Cora once told us with a sigh after catching a glimpse of herself in the hall mirror.

Cora had been a hospital nurse before she married Doc and moved to Foersterville. That's why Mom asked her to show the high school girls how to make bandages for the Red Cross hospital project.

Of course, Cora responded with her usual verve: "That would be great fun!"

She showed up just before the end of the school year, on the Friday before the New York State Regents exams—the last and most important tests of the entire school year. We got to take the whole afternoon off from our classes to work with Cora. It was a welcome break from cramming for our finals.

The girls were asked to stay in the cafeteria at the end of the lunch period and to spread out among all the tables so that we'd have plenty of room to work. We were just getting settled in our places when I heard the jingle of Cora's shoes in the hall outside. In she strode—with Vivian on her hip—followed by four boys who had volunteered to be her bearers. They carried two big cartons of muslin and gauze; a basket of scissors, pins, and other things we'd need to make the bandages; and a satchel that we all took to be a doctor's bag but that turned out to be full of things for little Vivian—mainly diapers. It was quite the procession.

Cora showed us how to disinfect our hands and the cafeteria tables and then demonstrated how to cut, layer, wrap, and fold the cloth to make tidy bandages. Then she walked among the tables to offer help when it was needed. I didn't know how she was able to do all that and deal with the baby at the same time. But as Ida says, Cora is a wonder.

As each of us completed our own bandages, we packed them into the cartons and helped the others with their work. My friend Rosie and I had worked quickly enough to have a little time toward the end of the session. We also had enough leftover scraps to make a special gift for both Cora and Vivian—half a dozen brand-new diapers. (This gesture was Rosie's idea. She adores Vivian and admires

Cora. I never would have thought of doing such a thing. I love Rosie's thoughtfulness.)

We slipped the diapers onto Cora's work table just before cleanup time. Cora seemed charmed by our gesture, but Vivian was unimpressed. So far as I could tell. But maybe someday . . .

Rosie and I, along with several other girls, helped stow all the boxes in Cora's roadster at the end of the class so that she could deliver them to the Red Cross office. I'm pretty sure she is the only woman in town who has learned to drive an automobile. We all admire Cora. She's a wonder. A Modern Woman.

10

On Monday we got a letter from Francis, written hastily in pencil on a few tiny sheets of paper torn from a notebook.

June 15

Dear Folks at Home,

The Sergeant tells us we've marched around enough here to get started on our advanced training. They'll be sending me and a couple of the other fellows up to artillery school in Vermont. The rest are heading to different camps all up and down the coast. I'll miss them all, especially Will! It's no surprise to me that they decided to send him to work at a hospital out by Syracuse. He's a smart and sensible fellow.

Before we go, we get a three-day leave! That's not long, but it's just enough time to come home for a couple of days. Will is coming with me. Mom, I promise we won't be any trouble. Will is a nice fellow, a real gentleman. We'll get in late next Friday and leave around midday Sunday.

Your loving son, Francis

PS—I'm sorry about the stationery. The little pad is small enough to carry around in my pocket, so I can dash something off whenever I get a spare minute.

I read that letter over and over all week long.

Francis! I'd missed him so!

And Will! What a surprise to get to meet him so soon! I'd missed Will too—I mean, if you could miss someone you hadn't even met yet.

But soon!

Friday finally came. Francis had said they'd arrive late, but I wondered, *When does "late" begin? It has to be after noon, but how long after?*

I supposed I could fake some minor illness to get out of school. Rosie does that all the time. She seems to know just how long to leave the thermometer in hot water so that it registers a plausible fever and her mother lets her stay home. Rosie is rather proud of that accomplishment. (I admit I tried it once and ended up with a fake fever of 106 degrees. Fortunately, I read the mercury before showing it to Mom. She'd never have believed me after that!)

I knew that if I were successful at being "sick," Mom would never let me get up to see the boys anyway. She would make me spend the whole weekend alone in my bed. So I'd just have to go to school and wait it out until dismissal time at 3:30. *Late* was unlikely to arrive before then anyway.

As soon as the final bell rang, I raced home. What a disappointment to find nobody new in the house, nothing changed—except for the aroma of roasting chicken in the oven. *Late* didn't happen during supper, either, nor through all the long evening afterward. After the last train from Albany passed through at 10:20, the family started drifting off to bed: first Lucy, then Pop, then Ida. Mom kept watch in the parlor. She always stays up until the last of us is safely home.

I tried to go to bed calmly, like Lucy. But I kept thinking about how much I missed my big brother—and, though I would never say so out loud, how much I longed to meet my admirer, Will. I counted sheep for a long time, but after a thousand or two, I concluded I'd never get to sleep. I wrapped the quilt around my shoulders and tiptoed along the upstairs hall to the small sitting area above the front door. It had a window that would let me look down onto Iroquois Avenue and anyone who approached the front door. I planned to wait and watch until the boys arrived.

I haven't any idea how late it was when they finally got here. Midnight? Two? Five? It seemed like an eon before I saw some dark shapes approach and heard scuffling on the front porch, Mom's excited whisper, the clunk of luggage in the hall, and the creaking of the staircase as the three of them made their way upstairs toward Francis's room at the front of the house, just across the hall from Mom and Pop's.

I stayed as quiet as I could. If it had been just Francis, I would have popped up from the chair and smothered him with my joy. But Will was with him. I didn't want Will to see me sleepy, in my nightgown.

"We would have been here sooner," Francis whispered as they came up the stairs. "We missed the last train and had to walk all the rest of the way from Holland Junction. No, Mom, we're fine. We got used to long walks in training." There was a smell that came with them, the masculine smell of sweat—and exhaustion. The light was dim. They didn't see me lurking in the shadows only a few feet away. I was glad to see and not be seen.

I caught a glimpse of the boys as they entered their room. Francis looked stronger, more erect than when I last saw him in April. He looked like a man. I couldn't say as I'd ever had a man for a brother before then.

Even in the dim light, I saw the elegance of Will's profile with a long, straight nose and smooth, almost translucent skin. He was lean, but taller than Francis. He looked more like an artist or a poet—or a prince—than a soldier. Oh my. I *did* want to know him better.

Mom yawned and headed across the hall to her room, passing me on the way. I worried briefly about being seen as she walked past me in the dark but then relaxed when I realized how tired she was. I waited, intending to sneak back down the hall and go to bed as soon as I could be sure everyone was asleep. The plan didn't work quite as I'd intended. I fell asleep in the rocking chair.

It was just dawn when I awoke. I crept back to my room and bedded down again without rousing Lucy.

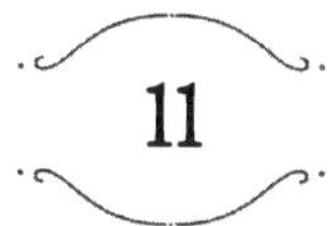

11

I didn't get up till late, but I wasn't the only one. When I rose, the boys were still snoring away in their bedroom down the hall.

What woke me was the tantalizing smell of ginger cookies in the oven downstairs. Lucy was already busy in the kitchen, I discovered as I headed for the icebox to make myself some breakfast. She had tossed a block of cream cheese into a mixing bowl and was mashing it when I passed by. She looked up. "Well, well, well!" she said. "Good morning, Ellie. You've been quite the lazybones today. I'm glad you're finally up! I can use your help getting ready for our big outing."

"Outing?"

"Yes, it came to me in the night. What better way could there be to celebrate Francis's visit—"

"And Will's."

"And Will's—than rowing up to Muller's Island for a picnic, just like the ones we used to have when we were kids?"

It crossed my mind that possibly, just possibly, she might have a motive beyond entertaining Francis and Will, but I held my tongue. After all, Muller's Island would be a romantic place to get to know Will—even though Reid did live there now.

"There's a jug of Ida's homemade grape juice chilling in the icebox, and I've baked a batch of cookies," she told me. "Now I'm working on two different sandwich fillings. Will you make the sandwiches for me while I pack the picnic basket?"

So I cut thin slices of bread for the sandwiches and spread them with Lucy's fillings—chicken salad made with last night's leftovers and cream cheese with olives and pimento. I made an extra one with both fillings layered together for my own breakfast. It was a tasty combination!

I had already started making up little packets of two sandwiches—one of each kind—and wrapping them neatly in waxed paper, when Lucy came over to supervise.

"We need *ten* sandwiches, not eight!" she said.

"Oh. Okay. I can make ten." It wasn't hard to guess why she needed ten sandwiches, but I kept my mouth shut. After all, Lucy already knew how I felt about Reid. The job took a little ingenuity, scraping just a bit of filling off each finished sandwich to make enough for two more. It would have been a good deal easier if I hadn't already used up the leftovers for my own gluttonous breakfast.

When the boys finally got up around noon, Lucy told them about her plan. They were happy to go along with it. They chose to forget about breakfast altogether and just head upstream with us, deciding to swim while we rowed along beside them. That was a good idea—it wouldn't have been easy to load all four of us, along with lunch, into the little pram.

What a glorious day, warm and sunny! Lucy and I dawdled along in the pram to stay with the boys as they swam upstream to Muller's Island. Francis, who had spent his whole life on the river, swam as if he'd been born in the water. Will moved more elegantly, like someone who had learned the proper style from a swimming teacher. He looked graceful as he moved through the water—dancing, you might say.

It was hard to believe that even these two good swimmers could be slower than the pram, which is the slowest rowboat I've ever seen. I wished we still had the sleek old skiff that I remembered from when I was younger. Boats should be pretty, fast, and fun to row, like the skiff. Of course, the little pram, with its blunt, flat bow and bathtub proportions, is anything but sleek. At least it was able to keep up with the boys, and we girls fulfilled our duty to make sure no one drowned along the way.

At the top of Muller's Island is a little wooded cove where visiting boats tie up. Once Lucy and I saw that the boys were safely ashore at the downstream end, we made our way to the cove and tucked into that little hideaway, tying up next to Reid's sagging old raft.

"Hey girls, are you there?" It was Francis's cheery voice.

We made the short, steep ascent through the brush to the meadow above, taking care to avoid the poison ivy along the way. Will and Francis, still soggy from their swim, were already waiting for us near the top as we climbed. They gallantly took the picnic basket and the bundle of clothing and towels from us as we got close.

At Lucy's insistence, the four of us made our way toward the little shed where Reid lives to let him know we were there—and invite him to lunch. As we approached, he rose up out of the plot of corn that he'd been weeding.

After Francis introduced him to Will, Reid offered to take us on a "house tour" of his neatly kept shed, which was furnished with a wooden bench and a narrow pallet on the floor. All four walls were lined with rough plank shelving that went all the way up to the tiny, high windows, and the shelves were crammed with scores of books. (Most had library markings on their spines, I noticed. Had Reid stolen them? I wouldn't be at all surprised.)

The books served a dual purpose, he told us: Besides offering plenty for him to read, they helped insulate the place at night. He figured he had enough books to last him until harvest. When he finished them all, he'd turn them back in at the library, then round up more to keep him warm and busy through the winter. Thelma, the town librarian, always has old, worn books in the cellar, he told us, and she is only too glad to turn them over to an enthusiastic volunteer like Reid. "She lets me keep the ones I want to read and return the old ones for her to pass on to the next impecunious scholar."

Impecunious. Evidently he likes big words. It was the first good thing I'd seen in him. And he wasn't a library thief after all. I would never admit it, but I was a little disappointed to learn that.

After the tour, we laid out Lucy's carefully prepared picnic lunch on the picnic table next to Reid's shack. There was just enough room at the table for the five of us.

Reid ate like a horse. He downed what seemed like half a gallon of grape juice and half a dozen cookies. I did what I could to hold back (not too hard, actually, after my giant breakfast) and leave enough for the others—especially, of course, Will, who may be too polite for his own good. He is a lean fellow, after all.

After lunch, Reid showed us around his farm. Besides the corn, which still had at least a month to go before it ripened, he had planted tomatoes, peppers, carrots, onions, lettuce, cabbage, and beans. They all looked as though they were thriving. "No deer on this island to eat the crops," he told us. "No woodchucks, no rabbits. This is the perfect spot to grow vegetables."

He pointed out the tangle of brambles—raspberry and blackberry bushes—by the edge of the woods, and in the meadow, the nearly invisible strawberry and huckleberry plants tucked in among the grasses.

"My best crops," he said, "are the ones I haven't planted at all.

They were growing here already, but no one ever harvested them for market. I can sell them for a fancy price at Johnnie's grocery store. It's funny—most of this stuff grows wild along back roads or in the cemetery, but the rich folks around here would rather buy their berries than pick them. Up on Yankee Hill, we've got to get out there fast before the neighbors—or the black bears—beat us to the harvest."

The strawberries were already ripening. Together we picked them and packed the fruit in pint cartons made of thin wood. It takes a lot of those little wild strawberries to fill a pint container. But all of us together managed to assemble twelve of those cartons, enough to make a full case, plus one more that Reid let us take to our family.

I resisted the urge to point out to him that we rich, lazy townies had just done his work for him this afternoon—and fed him too!

Then Lucy volunteered to drop the case of berries off at Johnnie's store on our way home.

"That's a heavy load! Let me help you carry it to the grocer's," Will proposed. What a contrast to Reid's oafishness. Lucy accepted Will's offer, so he carefully placed the flat of berries on the floor of the pram and squeezed the picnic basket in beside it. Will would row home with Lucy while I got to swim along with Francis.

Going back downstream is more of a float than a swim. It always makes me think of when we were children. Francis and Lucy and I had had a grand time as we drifted along on our backs, looking up at the lacy canopy of trees overhead, spraying water in the air to make rainbows in the sun. Or we'd see who could swim farthest underwater before coming up for air. Francis had always beaten us at that contest before, but he'd gotten out of practice in the army, and this time I could almost catch him. When we got tired of playing these old games from our past, we settled into a lazy sidestroke, facing each other, and had our first real talk since he'd arrived home.

"Are you glad you joined the army?" I asked him.

"Yeah, I was feeling boxed in at home. I'm glad I didn't wait for the draft—sure thing I'd be stuck in the infantry. The thought of spending the war in a stinking trench does not appeal to me. Artillery is more high-class."

"So you planned it that way?"

"Hell no! Oops, sorry for the language, El. I just wanted to get the—to get out of here, that's all. Don't tell anybody this, but I didn't know what I was getting myself into or how it would turn out."

"Did, um, Will?"

"I'm sure he did, though I never asked. Will is a real smart fellow. Did I tell you he was studying to be a doctor before he signed up? He wanted to treat wounded soldiers at the front, but I guess he's pretty satisfied with his assignment at the military hospital here in the States. You can ask him."

I certainly would.

Lucy and Will had already arrived at the boathouse and left to deliver Reid's cargo well before we got back. I guess they'd been so intent on doing that job that they forgot to keep an eye on us as we swam. Or else they knew that the two of us were such good swimmers that we didn't need an escort.

We grabbed our clothes from the pram and dressed quickly.

"Can you take the picnic basket home, Ellie?" he asked. "Tell the folks I've got an errand to run and will be back for supper."

We hugged each other as we parted. "What a grand day." We both said it at the same moment—a little ode to our joy.

12

I hadn't expected to be trudging up the hill all by myself, loaded down with the remains of our picnic in one arm and all our soggy towels in the other. I have to admit I was feeling a bit forlorn by the time I climbed the back stairs up to the kitchen.

Mom met me at the door. "What has become of the others?" she asked, looking worried. Mom has a real gift for imagining disasters.

She seemed quite satisfied with my explanation that Lucy and Will were delivering fruit to the grocer, but Francis's "errand" was another question. "Did he say where he was going? With whom? How long he'd be gone?"

"No, Mother. All he said was that he'd be back for supper."

"Did he go to the other side of the river? Did he take the boat?"

"I don't know. I wasn't looking."

Mom sighed. She still frets a lot about Francis. I don't know why; he's on his own now. I sometimes wish she'd worry more about me. But then . . . at least she's not interrogating *me* all the time about where I'm going or where I've been.

I washed up, changed clothing, and helped Mom and Ida prepare for supper. I'd just finished setting the table when Pop came in. Instead of settling in the parlor as he usually does, he sat down at the kitchen table while we worked around him. He seemed to enjoy our bustle.

"How was your day, Eleanor?" he asked. "Was your brother well? And what did you learn about this young fellow, Will Fox?"

"I had a fine time, Pop. I think the boys did too. Francis said he's glad to be in the army. He told me Will was studying to be a doctor before he volunteered. Will's a good swimmer. And polite."

"That will please your mother."

"Yes," said Mom. "He does seem like a nice young man. I'd like to know about his people, of course."

Pop sighed. "Of course."

Just then, Lucy and Will came in, flushed and merry. I wished I'd had a chance to go along with them on their errand—I wanted to know all about Will—but I was sure my chance would come soon.

Mom barely disguised her own effort to learn all about him and his people. "Are you planning to visit your family before you leave on your next assignment?" she asked graciously as soon as he joined us in the kitchen.

"Alas," said Will, "I have no family. My parents both died when I was a baby. My father caught diphtheria from one of his workers, and he passed it on to my mother. I was raised by my grandmother, but she's gone now too."

"Oh, poor dear! All alone!"

"On the contrary! I was lucky beyond measure to have been raised by such a kind and loving woman. She stayed with me until I was ready to make my own way, and I feel her presence to this day. She had been a teacher in her younger days—like you, Miss Klaus."

Ida nodded. It was interesting to me that Will already knew this about Ida even though he'd just met her. Maybe Francis had told him about her. Or maybe Lucy.

Francis didn't show up by suppertime. We waited as long as we could, but finally ran out of patience and sat down to eat. It wasn't until we were finishing our soup that Francis rolled in, looking a little sheepish—and smelling like a barnyard. Mom banished him to clean up as the rest of us sat around waiting for the next course. Then she started probing to see where he'd been all this time.

"I called on Bess Welk and her family across the river. It was just before milking time, so I went out with Bess to help bring in the cows. Along the way," he said, "we sat down for a while in the pasture to talk. It took us a while to get back, and then I couldn't leave before helping her with the milking."

Mom looked at him disapprovingly. I don't think she trusts Bess with her only son. I suspect that she has grander plans for Francis. Maybe someday a glamorous opera singer will take an interest in him.

The rest of the evening went quietly: another pleasant supper at home, followed by some enthusiastic singing around the piano. Lucy played hymns while the rest of us sang along—Mom on the soprano line, me at alto, Pop and Francis on baritone, and Will with a lovely tenor, exactly the voice part we had been missing in our family musicales. He fit right in.

The evening had to end early because Will would take the first train the next morning to his new hospital assignment. As we all said goodnight, Mom invited him to come back again soon. He seemed pleased to accept, and Mom looked pleased too. I thought, *Will likes us.*

I'd have to rise early in the morning to see him off.

13

The next day, Sunday, I overslept again. And once again, Lucy was already up and out of our room by the time I awoke. I jumped out of bed and dressed quickly to make sure I'd be ready in time to bid Will farewell. I caught the scent of an unfamiliar shaving soap—Will's?—as I raced past the bathroom on my way downstairs to catch up with him. The house was silent. There were a few signs of a hurried breakfast, but no people.

I was too late. Looking out the kitchen door, I saw Francis and Lucy walking back up the hill from the station. The whistle of the westbound train was already fading up the valley. I wouldn't get to say goodbye to my Will. *Damn.*

Lucy spotted me at the door. "Don't be so sad, Ellie! Next time, he's promised he'll be back for a whole week. We'll get to take him to the fair!"

Francis added his own words of encouragement. "And you still have *me*, little sister. I don't leave till after dinner."

The two of them were dressed for church—Francis in his crisp uniform, looking rather like Douglas Fairbanks. This was the first time I'd seen him as a soldier. Or a movie hero, come to think of it.

It was almost ten! I needed to get ready myself. It was a good day for the Easter dress, which had sat so long in the closet waiting for a real occasion. I wished Will could see me wearing it. But he'd be back soon, I knew. Maybe when I went to the station to meet him on his return . . .

Francis made a big splash at church. As soon as we walked in, I heard excited whispers throughout the congregation. Later, Pastor Warner worked Francis's noble bravery and patriotism into his sermon. And everyone crowded around Francis at the end of the service to welcome him home and wish him well in the trials to come. All that adulation would give most fellows a big head, but my brother seemed to handle it with grace.

John came over for Sunday dinner, bringing his camera with him. Before dinner, I helped him set up a group shot of the whole family on the front porch, with Francis kneeling next to Ida in her rocking chair and the rest of us standing around them. We also did a few portraits of Francis in his uniform, taken in the parlor when the light was just right. Portraits are a lot easier to do in the studio, where you can choose a simple background and a few artful props: a chair, a column, a bit of elegant drapery. At home, we had to clear out a bushel of bric-a-brac to get anywhere close to a comparable simplicity. But we did get two images that seem to have captured the essence of Francis as the proud soldier at home.

My brother didn't have to leave until four in the afternoon because Doc and Cora Baker, along with baby Vivian, would be coming by in their Franklin automobile to drive him all the way to Albany, where he would board the train to his new base up in Vermont. There was plenty of time for a farewell Sunday dinner that was a lot more peaceable than the one we'd had the last time we'd all been together, on the first day of our Great War.

The whole family gathered once more on the front porch, this time to bid Francis farewell.

Ida rose from her rocking chair to embrace him wordlessly.

Pop threw an arm around his shoulder, and Mom held him close. “Be careful, dear,” she said.

Lucy and I hugged him as if we’d never let go. “I’ll be back,” he assured us. “After all, I’m just going to Vermont!”

John shook his hand. “Take care of yourself, buddy.”

And then Francis was gone too.

PART THREE
IN LOVE

14

Just about everybody in our family has a specialty at the county fair. Mom always enters her baked goods—breads, cakes, and pies all made with flours from Pop's mill—and she usually gets at least one prize. Ida has her fancywork—knitted, quilted, sewn, tatted. She's had blue ribbons in all these crafts over the years. Recently, Lucy began entering her pretty embroidery, though she hasn't won yet. Francis once won a ribbon for a Rhode Island Red cock that he'd raised from egghood.

My specialty so far is not in the ladies' department or in animal husbandry but on the midway. I'm pretty good at aiming balls at targets and have won a fair number of teddy bears along the way. This is different from having an actual talent, but several of our young neighbors are very grateful to me for passing those bears on to them. This year, I was hoping to take home a gigantic one for baby Vivian.

The Iroquois County Fair always runs for a whole week at the end of August, just before school begins. The fair is a big draw for people from all over the county, and from as far away as Albany and Oneonta. Mainly they come by train, but these days we see more and more folks arriving in automobiles. Horses are getting downright rare as transportation, though we still see a few of them at the fair, coming in from the surrounding farms.

Pop is keen on the horse races that they run every afternoon—

trotters or pacers, depending on the day. I think he likes to bet on them, but he keeps quiet about it because Mom is dead set against gambling. As far as I know, he's never brought back a windfall from this little vice.

The strapping big draft horses are also there, competing to see which ones can pull the heaviest load. I'm fond of all the horses and always visit them in the stables. I love to stroke their velvet noses.

Cow's noses, on the other hand, are not strokable; they're hairless and wet. It's more fun to run your hand along their soft cheeks—and to offer them wads of hay, which they pull out of my hand with their long, rough tongues.

Pop always laughs at me for being sentimental and treating livestock as "house pets" instead of as useful farm animals that provide us with food and labor. I can't say I'm alone in that view; Francis's beloved rooster, Doodle, lived to a ripe old age instead of being served up as Sunday dinner, which had been the original intent. Even Pop shed a few tears when Doodle died. I saw them.

Our festivities started early this year—on Sunday afternoon, when Will's train came in from Syracuse. I intended to be at the station to meet him this time.

Sunday morning was busy, though. Mom had just finished making one of her specialties, a pear pie, to enter in the homemaking competition. The pie was still hot when she told me to run it down to the fairgrounds for the judges to taste it. The spicy aroma was tempting! But I have learned from Mom that you can't test a pie without spoiling its appearance, so I held back. She has always been a little intimidated about making pies for this reason, which is odd to me. She says you can taste the crumbs to find out whether a *cake* came out right, but there's no testing a *pie* before you serve it. As far as I know, though, Mom has never made a bad pie. And what *is* a bad pie, anyway?

As long as I was making deliveries, I took a few of Ida's preserves along to enter as well. I thought she deserved some recognition for her cooking as well as her fancywork.

The midway was just setting up when I arrived at the fairgrounds. The merry-go-round, the swings, and the Ferris wheel were half-constructed. The sideshow tents were up, and the workers were erecting garish billboards in front of them to advertise the acts inside. Smaller tents for games and food were going up in between.

The big red-and-gray homemaking building was just beyond the midway. It was full of busy women working to arrange the handicrafts along the walls and take in the foods they would have to sample and judge before tomorrow, opening day.

Just as I was passing the station on my way home, a train from the west pulled in—early. It was Will's train! I couldn't believe my good luck. I got to greet him just as he stepped off the train. It was all I could do to keep from taking him into my arms.

Instead, I helped him with his valise up the Verona Street hill to our front door. Ida was in her usual spot for a fine day, settled in her porch chair and concentrating on the batch of mending in her lap.

"Look who's here!" I hollered as we came close. I guess I was too loud and too sudden because she startled, pricking herself in the finger with her needle. Will leapt to her aid, pulling a clean handkerchief from his breast pocket and pressing it against the drop of blood on her finger.

She beamed at him. "My land, Will! What a gallant young fellow you are! Welcome back to Foersterville."

"Thank you, ma'am. I'm glad to be back!"

"Lucy will be surprised that you've arrived already. It can't have been more than a minute ago that she headed out the back door to meet you at the station. It seems you just missed connecting with each other."

"Oh no! We don't want to have poor Lucy cooling her heels for an hour down there, do we, Eleanor? Why don't you and I trot back down to meet her?"

We left Will's bag in Ida's care and back we went to the station. We found Lucy pacing on the platform, looking up at the station clock with each lap. It seemed not to have occurred to her yet to inquire about whether Will's train had been early.

Her face lit up when she saw us approach. Then she looked puzzled. Where was the train? Why was Will coming from the wrong direction? Why was I with him? We helped her solve this mystery. Then the three of us walked back up Verona Street with Will in the middle.

Mom probably would have thought that improper. She believes that gentlemen should always walk next to the curb. I once asked her why; she'd paused for a moment as if trying to remember, but maybe she'd just been trying to work out a delicate way of answering my question. Finally, she replied. "Ah, folks used to empty their chamber pots out of second-story windows into the street. The gentleman would protect the lady from being sullied . . . in that way."

"I've never *seen* a chamber pot emptied into the street. Have you?"

"Well . . . no, dear. But paying attention to the rules of etiquette is one way to know if a person is a true gentleman."

"I see. The rules are useful only because they let you know who takes them seriously, not because they serve any useful purpose."

"Eleanor, you are much too saucy for your own good. You need to attend to the rules of etiquette if you are to become a real lady. Or to marry a real gentleman."

I strongly suspected that Mom would have granted an exception to her rule in this case. After all, Will was with *two* ladies, not just one. I noticed that walking between Lucy and me allowed him to be equally attentive to both of us, which struck me as what a *real* gentleman would do.

Mom was waiting for us at the door. Her eyes were sparkling.

"I am delighted that you have chosen to honor us with your company," she said, embracing him. It was clear to me that she saw him as a real gentleman—whether or not he walks at the curb. So did I.

"*I'm* delighted," he responded. "And grateful—that you have chosen to welcome me into your home. Francis is a dear friend of mine, and I'm honored to know his charming family."

I sighed. I'm a member of that charming family.

Supper was a casual affair that hot Sunday night. We ate on the back porch, where we could catch the breeze wafting up from the river. Will was a lot more talkative than he had been on the last visit.

"And how has your training been going, Will?" Mom asked. "Have you had contact with actual patients?"

"I'm learning every day, Mrs. Foerster. In the hospital, I'm learning how to give tetanus shots and treat sprains, broken bones, and other wounds that fellows get in training. I'm also learning how to attend hospital patients with more serious wounds and infections. It's as if I'm already an intern even before I become a doctor!"

He continued, "In class, I'm learning about the kinds of battlefield decisions that medics have to make in the field—like triage, a way to divide patients into three groups—the gravely wounded, who will die no matter what you do to save them; the seriously injured, who need medical help to survive; and the rest, who will heal with or without medical intervention. It's a way of sorting out what you can do that will actually help someone and what you must leave to nature or fate."

He paused for breath, then added enthusiastically, "And I've learned how to use a tourniquet to stanch the flow of blood from a wound."

Mom cringed, but Ida smiled. "Sometimes, just a handkerchief will do the job," she said. "I *thank* you, Dr. Fox!" She gave him back his handkerchief, already washed and ironed after the pinprick on the porch.

"Will you be going off to the front?" Pop asked.

"I don't know yet, but I hope so. The experience would serve me well in my future career."

Nobody asked me, but I hoped *not*. It was hard enough to accept the idea that Francis might go off to war in Europe—which he was pretty likely to do. After all, he was learning to shoot big guns.

15

After that first night, the three of us—Lucy, Will, and I—spent most of the next five days at the Iroquois County Fair. We sampled all the foods we saw for sale: crisp waffles, frozen custard, cotton candy, taffy, hot dogs, fried chicken; we visited all the farm animals from chickens to oxen; we watched horse races, jugglers, high-wire acts, magicians, comedians, and bands; we saw the Home Guard performing their drills. It was all thrilling, but also exhausting. We needed an occasional break on the midway.

There was a new ride this year, the Whip. The three of us watched it for a while before deciding whether to ride. It looked quite tame at first, like a merry-go-round but without the horses or the brass ring. You sit in a car that goes around and around on a long oval track. What I didn't see at first was that the car makes a sudden jerk every time it goes around a curve. For me, that jerking motion was what made it interesting. I was ready to try it! Not Lucy, who has always shied away from things that are too fast or too unpredictable. But gallant Will was happy to go, and the ride was thrilling. What I enjoyed most about the Whip was being thrown so close against Will on those vigorous turns. I would have taken that ride with him again and again, but alas, Will was ready to try something else instead.

We moved on to the Ferris wheel, another ride Lucy had always stayed away from in the past. This time, she was prepared to go—but only if she got to sit in the middle, away from the great abyss on either side. I was happy with that since the abyss is what appeals to me. But then, she got to sit next to Will—and cling to him, I noticed.

The view from the Ferris wheel was lovely, with the river, the farms on the far side, and Yankee Hill rising above them. On the near side was the village and the lovely, tall steeple of our church. There was a haze of green from all the elm trees, maples, and chestnuts throughout the village and on the hills. There was a puff of smoke from an approaching train down the valley. *Why would anyone want to leave this beautiful place?* I wondered each time we reached the top of the wheel.

I pointed out all my favorite local sights as the wheel carried us up and down. Will enjoyed the scenery with me, but Lucy cowered between us, unwilling to open her eyes. I think she is something of a sissy, unlike the two of us.

After the Ferris wheel, Will agreed to go on the merry-go-round with Lucy. That's far too tame a ride for me. I chose to play games instead. I wandered through the midway, looking for the largest bear that I could win for baby Vivian. I found a beauty, two feet high, with blue button eyes and a soft, huggable coat of white fur. To win it, I had to hit four targets in a row with my ball. It took a while, but finally, I did it—just as Will and Lucy arrived from the merry-go-round. I don't know which was better, my winning the bear or their enthusiastic cheers.

On our way home, we delivered the bear to Doc and Cora. Vivian squealed with joy when she saw it.

We arrived home just in time to wash up for supper. It was hard to imagine that after all the food we'd consumed at the fair, we'd still have room left for chicken and biscuits at home. Ida has always said that young people have a bottomless capacity for food, and this time, I believed her.

After such a long and exciting day, we all retired early. As we got ready to go to bed, I noticed that Lucy was holding a ring of brass or bronze. It looked like a brass ring from the merry-go-round. She brushed it against her face, then tucked it into the little cedar box that she keeps by her bed—her "Treasure Box." She must not have had time to trade it for a free ride today. Probably she put it away so that she can use it next year.

"Good night, Little Sister," she whispered to me from her bed.

"Sleep tight, Big Sister," I replied from mine.

"Don't let the bedbugs bite!" we both chimed in together, in a bedtime ritual we've had since I was a baby.

Far too soon, fair week was over. Will headed off on the train, this time with our whole family there to say goodbye. Mom invited him to spend Christmas with us, and he looked delighted to accept. Francis was planning on it too—that is, if he wasn't in Europe by then.

After the train departed, the rest of the family headed straight home. But Lucy and I went the other way on Iroquois, toward Mr. Lloyd's stationery shop. School was about to begin, and we needed to do some important business to get ready for it.

16

The bell on Mr. Lloyd's door jingled as Lucy and I stepped inside the store. I heard his muffled voice from the back room.

"I'll be right with you!"

"No need, Mr. Lloyd. We know where everything is. We'll let you know when we're ready to pay for our things."

"Much obliged, Lucy!" He recognized her voice. He recognizes *all* the voices of Foersterville folk.

I picked out the routine things first: a couple of number two pencils, an eraser, a new nib for my fountain pen, a bottle of ink. Then I went on to the best part—paper. I chose five new notebooks, one for each class—composition books, black with white speckles all over. Pop calls them Holstein books because they remind him of dairy cows. Those clean, new notebooks with their crisp pages and fresh smell always feel like a whole new beginning to me. They make me hope that I'll learn something exceptional in the new school year.

Lucy would graduate in June. For her, the school year would be full of celebrations. For me, it was just challenges; eleventh grade was the year of trigonometry, physics, and the orations of Cicero.

As we walked home along Iroquois, we were surprised by Reid, who caught up with us from behind. He seemed about to pop with excitement. "Did you see all my prizes at the fair? I can hardly believe it! I won *five* blues and a red—every one of my vegetables won a ribbon!"

In fact, I hadn't seen any of the vegetable displays; I've never regarded vegetables as one of the high points of the fair, though I'm too polite to say that to Reid. I held my tongue. But Lucy came through, of course. "How marvelous for you, Reid! You must be very proud."

He glowed. Obviously, it was the right thing for her to say—even though, as far as I could tell, she'd never looked into the vegetable display either. Lucy is good at being sweet, if not entirely truthful.

All those prizes had led Johnnie, the grocer, to propose featuring Reid's produce, he told us. "Johnnie wants to label them all as special and charge extra for them. He wants to call my little farm 'Reid's Eden.'"

"A charming name," said Lucy. "So apt!"

I thought of our idyllic day there with Will. "Not bad," I had to admit.

School started right after the fair. Since Reid lived down on the river, he had to walk past our house every day on his way to school. It seemed like four days out of five, he showed up just as Lucy and I stepped off the front porch. I wondered if he had been waiting for her.

Lucy and Reid were in fourth-year Latin class together. This was their year to study Virgil's *Aeneid*. For Lucy, Latin was nothing but drudgery. She took it only because Mom felt strongly that it would teach her about English grammar and vocabulary. As a Latin student myself, I had found little evidence to support that. Maybe next year.

Reid, on the other hand, seemed to downright break into song on the subject of Latin. The *Aeneid*, he said, had some "damn good yarns in it."

"How do you know?" I asked. "You're just starting the class."

"I read the whole thing in English over the summer."

"Used a trot, eh?"

"Hardly! This was an English translation done by Dryden—over two hundred years ago—who turned it into an *English* poem—not just a transcription of a Latin one. If I used Dryden as a trot I'd be in trouble with Miss Blake for sure! But being familiar with the story will certainly help me focus on the language it's written in. Knowing is better than not knowing."

"But isn't that cheating, in a way?"

"Let's say you saw a performance of, say, *The Tempest* before you studied it in English class. Would that be cheating?"

"But wait! The school put on *The Tempest* just last year. Lucy was Ariel."

"And I was Caliban. You will study that play this year. Is it cheating that you've already dipped a toe in it?"

I had to admit he was probably right, at least about *The Tempest*. Knowing—or learning before you have to—is not the same thing as cheating. It may well be better than not knowing.

I had never seen such a Latin enthusiast as Reid. He'd even memorized a good portion of the material he'd read; he could spout forth in classical Latin at the drop of a hat. When I told him I was beginning Latin III, he responded instantly, in a stentorian voice, "*Quo usque tandem abutere, Catilina, patientia nostra?*" Something about . . . abusing . . . our patience? Whatever it meant (and I'd find out soon enough), Reid not only studied his Latin before starting the course but also *memorized* it afterward. This boy was odd!

17

The more I heard about what Lucy was studying in Latin IV, the more I wished I were in her class instead of mine, Latin III, which was filled with two-thousand-year-old political speeches. My class was reading Cicero, a famous orator. Cicero, it appears, was dead set on destroying Catiline, who seemed to have been a sort of union organizer of his day. I found myself rooting for Catiline, the underdog, but feared he would get it in the end.

Lucy, though, was studying this grand love story. She told us a little about it at the supper table one night.

Mom lit up when she heard the tale. "There is an obscure old opera by Henry Purcell about this very legend," she said excitedly. "I studied the opera years ago in conservatory, thinking that perhaps we could mount its very first production in America. We never did put it on, but I know I still have the piano score. It's somewhere down cellar, I believe."

The next morning, after rummaging for an hour among boxes of her old papers, she emerged triumphantly from the cellar adorned with cobwebs and bearing a big, musty volume bound in paper. *Dido and Aeneas*. "Here it is! I'll need some time to review this score. It's worth another look."

That night at dinner, Mom told us the whole story of the opera: Aeneas escapes from Troy when it is destroyed by the Greeks. The gods have told him he is destined to build a new city, Rome. He passes through Carthage on his way there. Dido, the queen of Carthage, welcomes him; when he tells her about his adventures along the way from Troy, she is so impressed that she falls in love with him. This is a dilemma for her because she has all these queenly duties in Carthage and he is fated to go found Rome. She decides to keep her love a secret because there seems to be no way for them to stay together while fulfilling their responsibilities. So then Aeneas leaves and Dido kills herself. And that's the end of the story.

It occurred to me that if Dido had thought about it, she would have realized her country would have had the same problem whether she ran off with Aeneas or killed herself. After all, either way Carthage would have to find itself a new queen. I wonder why she didn't think of that?

Mom had an answer. "Poor Dido wasn't half so clever as you, I suppose," she told me. "Besides, she would have lost the chance to perform a ravishing aria at the end. A death scene aria is the *sine qua non* of serious opera."

Mom sang the aria for us. It is beautiful, but Dido's decision still seemed foolish to me.

As we looked at the rest of the opera, one of Dido's arias nearly broke my heart. This one comes earlier, when Dido first falls in love with Aeneas. She feels a duty to keep her love a secret, but at the same time longs to tell him. Instead, she confides in Belinda, her best friend.

According to Mom, I have the right voice for Dido, a mezzo-soprano—unlike most opera heroines, who have higher voices. (I think *mezzo-soprano* is a fancy term for alto.)

I knew I must sing this song for Will at our next family chorale. It was the only way I'd dare tell him how much I care for him without the impropriety of being too blunt. I asked Mom to teach me to perform it like a real singer. She seemed puzzled at first, seeing that I had never expressed much interest in singing before now, but she was glad to take me on as her pupil.

I worked hard on the aria all during the fall, preparing it for a family musicale at some time in the future:

Ah, Belinda, I am prest
with torment not to be confessed.
Peace and I are strangers grown.
I languish till my grief is known
yet would not have it guessed.

It wasn't until after Thanksgiving that I dared to tell Mom of my intention to sing it at Christmastime. What I didn't mention was why it was so important for Will to hear it.

"But dear!" she said, horrified. "That musicale is a *Christmas* performance! It is certainly not a program devoted to pagan romance. Such tales are for the opera house . . . or for an ordinary recital. Your aria, pretty as it is, would be far beyond the scope of our holiday songfest!"

I persuaded her to let me sing it as a sort of encore at the very end of the program. I told her I wanted to show the whole family how much I'd progressed as a singer under her tutelage. She was able to accept that argument. What a relief.

Of course, the aria couldn't be my only present for Will, especially since he wouldn't know for certain that it was a gift to him. Mom suggested that Lucy and I knit special army items for him and Francis, things that would fit with the rest of their uniforms. Her Red Cross chapter had a whole book of patterns, all quite simple, that we could choose from. Lucy picked a high-necked jersey for Francis, a scarf and warm gloves for Will. I chose socks for Francis, and for Will a sweater vest with buttons up the front. There was nothing fancy about any of this fancywork; it all had to be in a dull olive color to match their uniforms, and we couldn't play with interesting stitch patterns because army men all had to dress alike. Mom said that each of the boys would know that his gifts had been handmade just for him, and he'll treasure them when he goes off to war.

Since creative knitting was forbidden, I came up with another way to put a little bit of myself into the project for Will. Alongside the yarn, I knitted strands of my own hair into his sweater. I decided not to tell him about it just now, but maybe someday . . .

18

Francis got home Saturday night for the whole week of Christmas. It was the first he'd been back since summer. Looking at him, I began to understand what people mean when they say someone has "military bearing." It's not just that he stood up straighter than he used to, or that he had stronger muscles, or that he looked so handsome in his uniform. Even out of uniform, he looked like a man of pride and confidence. A man to take seriously.

Sunday afternoon, he and Lucy and I went off to the Muller farm to collect a Christmas tree. The Mullers have a grove of firs they planted along the road that passes their farm. Every year, they mark a few that need to be cut to thin the planting, and they tell the villagers we can cut them as Christmas trees. It's a generous gesture, one that wins the neighbors' goodwill and provides the Mullers with a free service. Pop is impressed by their genius in accomplishing both at the same time.

We found a fine tall tree for the entry hall, where we all gather on Christmas morning to open our presents. As we were getting ready to haul it away, Lucy spotted a smaller one by the side of the road and suggested that we offer it to the Bakers. Cora, she said, had told her they were too busy this year to collect one for themselves. It was quite a trudge for the three of us to get both trees across the river and up Verona Street, but one look at the delight on the faces of Doc,

Cora, and even baby Vivian made the extra effort worth it. This was Vivian's first Christmas. That girl needed a tree!

On Sunday night, we set up our tree in the front hall and brought down boxes and boxes of ornaments from the attic to hang on the tree. Mom cautioned us to arrange the decorations carefully, but of course everybody in the family had a different idea of what a "careful arrangement" meant. We finally agreed on Pop's program of placing the ornaments first, with the ones that have the highest sentimental value in front; then filling in gaps with candy canes and ribbon candy; and finally, hanging tinsel icicles as a finishing touch. "Don't *throw* them at the tree!" Mom urged us. "Hang them *carefully*, one at a time!"

When the job was done, we all settled down—perched on chairs, sitting on stairs, and stretched out on the floor—to relax and admire our work as we sipped Ida's festive eggnog and devoured Christmas cookies. The doorbell rang.

Will!

We hadn't expected him until the next day. Francis, who hadn't seen him since they were transferred to different bases last summer, jumped up to embrace him and tote his bags up to their room. Ida fetched him a cup of eggnog, and Pop pulled in another chair from the dining room. Mom and Lucy beamed with delight. I was struck dumb by his sudden appearance. I hope I smiled at him with my eyes.

Monday was Christmas Eve, always a hectic day. There's much to do in the kitchen to prepare for the big feast on Christmas, so we don't have much time for socializing. Pop spent the morning working down at the mill while Francis squired Will all around town to introduce him to his friends. I would not be at all surprised if Bess Walk and her family were among them.

After supper, we all piled our presents under the tree, then walked up Verona Street to church for the evening service. This was the first time Will had been to our church, and of course everyone was curious to meet him and speculate about why he was staying with us instead of "going home to be with his family." They didn't realize that *we* are his family.

On Christmas morning, John showed up early (just after Santa Claus, he said) and added his own load of gifts to the great pile under the tree. Then all eight of us settled onto chairs and stairs for a sort of picnic breakfast in the front hall before opening our presents.

I waited until the very end to open my gift from Will. It was a slender book of poems, some of them quite long, by a person named Edna St. Vincent Millay. I had to work to conceal my disappointment. I don't like poetry! It's too pretentious. It seems to me that you can express the same ideas better in plain speech than in the fancy language of, say, *Evangeline*, which is a good story obfuscated by all those rhythms and rhymes. I shocked my English teacher when I said that in class. She made me write the whole story in prose to test my theory. I have to admit that it fell a little flat, but after all, I'm not a real writer like Longfellow.

I was leafing through the pages of Will's gift book when a card fell out. A special note from Will! Maybe that was the real gift.

Dear Eleanor,
This young poet reminds me of you:
a clever girl, a girl of strong opinions,
a thoroughgoing romantic at heart.
I hope you enjoy Miss Millay's work as much as I do.
Happiest of Christmases to you.
From your friend,
Willard Fox

If Will likes these poems, I thought, *maybe they are worth reading.* I'd look at them as soon as things quieted down after the holiday.

Dinner was planned for four o'clock, but before then was our family musicale. I was so excited about singing my love song to Will that I barely paid attention to the hymns and carols that came beforehand—except for Mom's solo. I always love to hear her pure soprano voice, but whenever she performs "O Holy Night," she sounds like an angel.

My own solo, "Ah, Belinda," came at the very end of the program. Mom had showed me how to make an aria come alive before an audience: memorize the music, look into the eyes of the audience, and make my face and body reflect the character's emotion. Then she'd helped me tone the emoting down for our small family audience. I felt ready. At last, it was time for my big moment.

I took a deep breath. Looked forlorn. Listened for the first four notes of the bass line. Then I came out with the aria's great opening sighs: "Ah! Ah! Ah! Belinda, I am prest with torment . . ." From there on, the music and the character took over. I became Dido herself. I sang feelingly. I looked longingly for comfort from my best friend Belinda (in this case the audience, especially Will). I reached out for succor. And the whole time, that steady bass line kept reminding me that this was not just drama but also music, and highly structured music at that. There was a fine tension between being carried away with Dido's passion and performing her musical duty.

I did a bang-up job, if I say so myself. My little audience cheered. John handed me a bouquet. (Ida quickly returned it to the dinner table, where she had originally placed it as a centerpiece.) I got warm hugs from Francis and Lucy, a kiss from Ida, an enthusiastic pat on the back from Pop, a proud look from Mom.

Will looked me in the eye, gently took my hand between his own, and said, "As you sang, I couldn't help thinking about all the young men who are leaving their girls behind in order to win this war. Thank you for reminding me, Eleanor, of the grief of those women."

I had been hoping he'd tell me that he loved me passionately, but this wasn't bad. I guess.

Now it was time for dinner to take over our attention. Mom, Ida, and Lucy did the last-minute cooking while Francis and I set the table and John brought out the first course. Pop and Will stayed in the parlor, waiting for dinner. Then Mom excused herself, and ten minutes later, so did Lucy. The four of us who were left did the final preparations and had everything ready for them when they came out of the parlor.

We all sat down at the table: Pop at the head with the Christmas turkey, Mom at the foot with the vegetables, and the rest of us in between.

Pop led the grace. Afterward, he remained standing instead of carving the turkey as he had always done before. He cleared his throat. "I have wonderful news for you all," he said. "Today our lovely daughter Lucy has agreed to marry young Will Fox. Let us all wish them well in their new life together!"

Francis jumped up. "Welcome to the family, brother!"

Lucy looked proud as punch, especially when Will rose to embrace her.

I went mute with jealousy and rage and shame. How could I have missed the signs of their growing fondness for each other? How could I have had the hubris to think that Will might favor a girl like *me*, not yet even sixteen years old? I love both Will and Lucy dearly; how could I be so resentful of their happiness together? Did Will know my song was just for him? Was he secretly laughing at me? Oh, the humiliation!

At dinner, I couldn't talk without fear of screaming or bursting into tears. I couldn't eat without fear of throwing up. I just pushed my food around the plate until I could no longer bear the excited conversation around me. Then, pleading a stomachache, I took off up the back stairs to our bedroom. On the way, I overheard Mom telling the others, "Ah, yes, I remember getting a case of nerves like Eleanor's after I debuted as a soloist. It took away *my* appetite too." At least Mom didn't know what really troubled me.

I threw myself on the bed and sobbed for what seemed like hours. I never knew I had so many tears in me.

After some time, Ida came to my side. "Pressed with torment, are you, my dear?" she asked gently as she rocked me in her arms. I couldn't talk through the tears. She held me close until I was too exhausted to cry anymore.

"I thought he loved *me*," I said.

"He does, dear. He loves us all. And we all love him. He had become part of our family even before he and Lucy decided to get married."

"But *me*! I thought *I* was the one he loved most of all. After all, I was the one he called 'that handsome girl' when he first saw me at the station."

"I think I understand, Eleanor. A stranger's compliment can cast a powerful spell, especially when the stranger turns out to be as dear a young man as Will has shown himself to be. I'm not surprised you were so enchanted that you missed the signs of his growing attachment to Lucy. I see your current grief, my girl. I know you have the strength in you to transform this disappointment into wisdom, but it will take time."

"I'll try, Belinda."

She smiled quietly. "I'll be right beside you all the way, Dido."

She held me until I fell asleep at last.

19

Right after the New Year, we started back to school. This would be Lucy's last term at Foersterville High before graduation—and marriage, which I supposed would come right afterward. June, they say, is the most romantic month for a wedding.

Reid was waiting for us near the corner, as usual, when we left the house on that first Monday morning after the holidays. *That boy is going to be disappointed*, I thought as we stepped off the porch.

I would have expected her to beat around the bush for a bit before telling him of her engagement, just to soften the blow. But Lucy wasted no time breaking the news: "Will asked me to marry him, and I said yes!" Of course I looked at Reid's face for any sign of disappointment or woe. He showed no sign whatsoever.

"I've seen it coming for quite a while," he said calmly. "You two are a very good match, in my opinion. You make me think of Doc and Cora Baker, two kind people who never have to think about being kind. I wish you every happiness together."

That response was not what I had expected. So was Reid *not* in love with my sister, or was he just covering up his disappointment? If he was disappointed, he was a lot better at hiding it than I was. I think the secret to keeping my *own* secret was not my personal self-control but that everyone in the family was too excited about Lucy's engagement to pay much attention to me. Except for Ida, of course. I was glad that she paid attention—and didn't let everyone in on what she saw.

"When are you planning to tie the knot?" he asked. "Right after graduation in June, I presume?"

"We haven't decided yet, Reid. On the one hand, we're eager to go ahead with it. On the other hand, though, it doesn't seem right to celebrate like that in the middle of a war. We may wait and marry when the war is over."

"I understand. I may have to hold off on my plans too. I *want* to start college in September—if I've saved enough money by then—but I can't risk that until after we win the war, lest I get dragged away into the army before I can find another reason to keep the draft at bay."

Interesting, I thought. *They talk to each other like good friends, not like sweethearts. I guess Lucy got over her crush on him.*

Reid told us he'd spent Christmas up on Yankee Hill with his family. This morning, he was wearing a jersey he told us his mother had knitted for him with wool from the family sheep.

"It's beautifully made," I said, admiring the intricate cable pattern.

"And warm, and waterproof!" Reid added. "It's just what I need in my little hovel down on the river. Of course, my mother—like yours, I'm sure—knows all about how to manage life in a hovel."

If Mom does know such things, she would never admit it, I thought. It had never occurred to me before this moment that my own mother had much in common with Reid's. It's hard to remember that she grew up poor too.

In school that day, I kept finding my attention drifting away from the work at hand toward my huge disappointment at Christmas. Tears kept welling up in me; it took all my concentration to keep them down. I spent a lot of time in the girls' room—enough to make a couple of my teachers ask if I was ill. It took all my strength to keep from breaking down in front of them.

Thank goodness for dear old Rosie. She found me sobbing in the bathroom at the end of the day and wrapped her arms around me.

"Is it Francis?" she asked gently.

I almost said no, but then thought better of it. What would Rosie think if I told her I was in unrequited love with my sister's fiancé? Besides, it's no lie to say I'm worried about my dear brother. Her affectionate concern gave me comfort, even though she didn't understand why I needed it.

When I got home, there was a new missive from Francis on the dining room table. He had been getting increasingly impatient since he transferred to the artillery training camp last summer. Recently, he'd been sending us note after note about how frustrated he was at having to wait so long to go off to war. It seemed he could barely hold back on profanity. In some places, you could see gaps where he must have erased it. Good thing he wrote in pencil. Mom would never approve of what he'd started to say:

We've been at war for almost a whole—year!

I've practiced my wartime skills until I am—blue in the face!

When will they let me loose to show that—Jerry what I can do?

Today's note began the same way:

There's still no news about deployment for us. It is—hard for a fellow to wait, and wait, and then wait some more to show what he is made of!

I do hope, though, that I'll get home again at the end of March for Easter and a week with the family, and again at the end of June for Lucy's graduation.

I was glad there were no erasures in that last sentence. I always look forward to seeing my big brother again—even if it's only every few months. The anticipation helps calm my mind.

This damn war was making it hard for all of us to make any plans, from a short visit home to going off to college to even getting married! I couldn't *wait* until it ended.

PART FOUR
HEALING

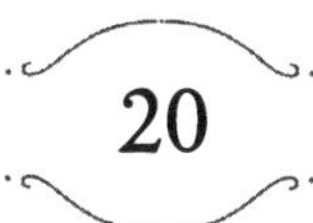

20

"I've *got* to have a room of my own!" The voice jolted me awake. I looked around the dark room to find the speaker; no one was there but Lucy, still fast asleep in her bed across the room. So the voice must have been my own, in a dream.

It had been almost a month since Lucy's engagement to Will, but she still badgered me every night with her tales of how *sweet* Will is and how *charmingly* he proposed to her and what a *beautiful* wedding they'll have when the Great War is finally over and how she can't *wait* to start a *family* with him and on and on and on. She took to wearing her brass ring from the merry-go-round on a golden chain around her neck, and she loved to tell me how Will had presented it to her. Over and over again.

I couldn't listen to her without having to hide my tears. And I couldn't say anything back without the risk of losing control and bawling out loud. She must have thought I'd gone mute.

I was just going crazy.

After my dream, when morning came, I started looking around the house for a new place to sleep, a place of my own. The attic was out. The ceiling was too low, and a family of bats had long since set up housekeeping there. I wouldn't want to share a room with them any more than with Lucy.

There was only one other place for me to go.

A hundred years ago, when our house was still an inn, the second floor had four big bedrooms, one at each corner. But a good half of one of those rooms had been taken over as a bath when the family got indoor plumbing. The remaining part of the old bedroom became a storeroom that filled up with dusty old books and magazines, disused furniture, and the old, outmoded clothes that we liked to use as Halloween costumes. That little room, I thought, might have possibilities.

I borrowed one of Ida's measuring tapes and undertook to survey the storeroom. My own single bed would fit perfectly along one wall—the wall with a window looking down onto Verona Street. There was space for my dresser between the bed and the doorway across the room. The wall at the back of the house had a dormer window that had a view of the river. The dormer formed a nook just the right size for a desk. Perfect.

My only problem was that the little room was full of other people's things. How could I get all that stuff out of the way?

The bulkiest item was the big four-poster bed, disassembled, that leaned against the wall where my dresser should be. There was another odd wooden frame against the same wall. I couldn't tell what it was. I asked Ida.

"Why, dear, that is the frame for the canopy of the four-poster bed. Your grandmother stripped off the drapery before she took the bed apart to make space for the bathroom. The fabric was worn to shreds by then."

"I wonder if Lucy would like to have that bed—if, say, she had our old room to herself."

"What makes you ask, Eleanor?" She seemed a little concerned, though I'm not sure why.

I told her about my daily torture, listening to Lucy chatter and swoon, and about how I longed to have the little room all to myself but didn't want anyone to know why. She sighed and smiled. "It seems that *each* of you is ready for her own private room," she said. "Why don't you sound Lucy out on the matter of the four-poster? I shall be glad to help if I can."

That night, as Lucy and I were preparing for bed, I took the first step. "I see you're starting to put together your trousseau. You already have the big stack of tea towels that Ida embroidered for you, and you're bound to collect more stuff. Do you know that there's a big bureau in the storeroom? We could move it in here so you can put all your wedding treasures in one special place."

"Lovely idea!" she said. "I may gather a lot if we have to wait until the end of the Great War before we finally get married."

She and I dragged that big old bureau over to our room. It didn't fit very well among all the other furniture, but we could work around it. And the little room had one less obstacle in it.

A few days later, I mentioned the bed. "You saw the canopy bed in the little room? I think it was our grandparents' marriage bed." I didn't know any such thing, but it did seem plausible. Plausible enough.

That night at dinner, without any more prompting from me, she asked Mom and Pop if she might have it as part of her trousseau.

"Of course you may," said Pop. "It's been sitting there unused for twenty-five years."

"I could make a new canopy for it," Ida offered, "but the bed would need to be set up so that I could fit it properly."

"Let's put it in our room!" I suggested. "I'd be happy to move my bed and dresser across the hall to make a space for it—at least for the time being."

So bit by bit, the stored things got transferred out of the storeroom, and my own little room started to take shape. We gave the old books and magazines to the library, and I took the Halloween costumes to an empty trunk in the attic. I found an old oaken table up there, which I carried down to use as a desk; it fit perfectly in the dormer alcove.

Meanwhile, Lucy took on her own bedroom project. She started sleeping in the trousseau bed and chose a white dotted Swiss fabric for the new canopy with a lining of pink silk taffeta. Ida stitched it up for her in no time, and she made pretty new window curtains to match the canopy. I helped Lucy move her single bed up to the attic for storage. Our old room was beginning to look quite romantic; Lucy seemed very happy with it.

And I got my own snug room at last. I never tired of watching from my bed as people came and went along Verona Street, and from my desk, I could see the whole sweep of our back lawn down to the river and the railroad beyond.

I decided not to hang up my favorite photograph, the one of Will and Francis and me at the train station. I took it out of its frame and placed it face down in the top drawer of my dresser. That way, I wouldn't have a constant reminder of what I'd lost.

No, not lost. I'd been dreaming. He and Lucy had awakened me. Ida tells me that the pain will fade one day. Meanwhile, I have my room. I'm so pleased to have this room that I sometimes lose track of why I needed it in the first place. That is, until the sadness sweeps me away again. Then I'm glad for the privacy.

One of the first things I chose to do with my privacy was to open the little book of poetry that Will gave me for Christmas, *Renascence and Other Poems*. It took me a while to decide whether to be delighted or shocked by Edna St. Vincent Millay. She writes about actually being in bed with a lover—or maybe with love itself—it wasn't entirely clear to me which. I did know, though, that I wouldn't show the book to Mom, who would be aghast at its naughtiness and then take it away from me. I slipped the book under the mattress, where *she'd* never look—but where I could retrieve it easily.

The more I read of Edna's poems, the more she seemed like an intimate friend, the kind you could tell anything to without fear of shocking her. Lord knows she didn't hold anything back from me. I may not have approved of her behavior (or what her poems suggested about her behavior), but Oh! She touched the pain I was feeling.

I copied out her "Sonnet II" onto a piece of notebook paper, waited till the tearstains dried, then tucked it under the photograph I had hidden in my bureau:

Time does not bring relief; you all have lied
Who told me time would ease me of my pain!
I miss him in the weeping of the rain;
I want him at the shrinking of the tide;
The old snows melt from every mountain-side,
And last year's leaves are smoke in every lane;
But last year's bitter loving must remain
Heaped on my heart, and my old thoughts abide!
There are a hundred places where I fear
To go,—so with his memory they brim!
And entering with relief some quiet place
Where never fell his foot or shone his face
I say, "There is no memory of him here!"
And so stand stricken, so remembering him!

21

After the holidays, I started to spend a lot more time away from home. The whole house was too full of Will, even my own little room. At first, I tried going to the village library right after school. But all that quiet and all those books gave me no peace. Every book was about Will. Every silence was full of him.

What I needed was someone to keep me company.

So I asked Rosie if we could start walking home from school together. Most days, we'd walk right past our house and head up Verona to her family's place next to the creek. Sometimes, on warmer afternoons, we would make our way up the creek bed itself from rock to rock. When I think back on it, I wonder how we avoided breaking bones. We did get wet and cold from time to time, but nothing worse than that.

I love Rosie's house. It isn't an old foursquare Colonial like ours but a more "modern" place, built not long after the railroad came through in the 1860s. I've always thought of it as a fairy-tale castle because of its rounded tower rising three stories over the front door. The tower room on the second floor, just above the porch, is a sewing room. The next two levels above it, joined by a spiral staircase, are Rosie's own. How I've always envied her that little apartment!

Most days we did our homework together. But sometimes we'd make up stories—like creating our own silly melodrama about two characters, dashing Marmaduke and wilting Bedelia. Bedelia was always getting herself into terrible fixes, like being stranded on an ice floe drifting off to sea. Then Marmaduke donned his cape and came to her rescue. Sometimes we switched their roles, making Bedelia the heroine who saved Marmaduke from one dilemma after another. I think I like this version better.

Rosie and I always had fun with Marmaduke and Bedelia. For me, the best thing about our game was that there was no Will in it.

I kept Will to myself.

22

Will came back to our house for Easter weekend. Rosie was there when he arrived. I thought she would never stop swooning. "Oh, Ellie! Why have you never told me about this? Will is so adorable! So handsome! So sophisticated! I almost wish he weren't engaged to your sister. I'd like to have him for myself!"

It was all I could do to keep from telling her to shut her mouth. I kept quiet and was relieved when she went home at last.

Oh dear. I had a sinking feeling that "Marmaduke and Bedelia" would turn into "Will and Rosie." Even Rosie's tower would no longer be safe for me.

I managed to contain myself by keeping my mouth shut while Will was visiting us, but Lucy showed no more self-restraint than Rosie. She held onto his arm the entire time, beginning Friday afternoon when the two of them went off together to talk with Pastor Warner. Planning the wedding, I suppose.

I kept my teeth clenched the whole time he was here.

Saturday morning after breakfast, Mom brought out our most recent letter from Francis and read part of it aloud to Will:

> *I'm sorry to let you down, folks, but it seems there's no point trying to make plans, not when a fellow is in the army. I won't be able to come home next month after all. Things are*

> *so busy around here that I may not even get a chance to write for a while. Don't worry, though, folks. I'm fine and raring to go. As the song says, "I don't know where I'm going, but I'm on my way!"*

"Does this mean what I think it does?" she asked.

"I can't say for certain, Mrs. Foerster, but I should not be surprised to hear that he leaves soon for the front."

"Just as I feared. I had hoped the war would end before that happened." Mom's face was wooden, expressionless, as she turned back to her writing desk and put the letter back in the drawer. I'd seen that look before when she was trying to maintain her composure in a crisis. There was a long silence.

Lucy broke it when she took Will by the hand and offered to show him her trousseau. Mom quickly broke out of her frozen state and began to laugh indulgently. "My dears, you must remember that it's highly improper for a young lady to escort a young man, even her fiancé, to her bedroom—unless, of course, they have a responsible chaperone." She rose and joined them on their way upstairs to look at the growing collection of linens and porcelain and cooking pots that was filling up Lucy's room: "Such stuff as dreams are made on," according to Ida. She said she was quoting Shakespeare.

My own dreams had been less of a problem than I'd expected during Will's Easter visit. I was learning ways to distract myself from pointless longing. One was to repeat under my breath the phrase "not mine" over and over, faster and faster, whenever I found myself getting upset. Pretty soon, "notmine, notmine" turned into "notma, notma" and then "namanama" as I got used to saying it. Lucy told me I seemed a little distracted, and she was right. But the distraction was worth the prize—keeping my emotions under firm control all through the visit, at least so far. I was pretty sure I could get through the whole weekend without making a scene. But I was ready to be by myself for an hour or two, and since they were busy with the housewares exhibit upstairs, I had my chance to escape. I pulled on my galoshes, grabbed a coat, and headed for the back door.

Ida was in the kitchen. She looked up from her work as I passed by. "Is all well?" she asked quietly.

I thought for a second, checking my interior. "I can manage, Ida. It's not as hard as I'd feared."

"You are stronger than you thought, my dear."

The backyard was still mostly covered with snow, though it had begun to melt in a few sheltered spots that got some sun. In the middle of one of these patches, I noticed a green leaf poking up from the soil—not a blade of grass but the broader leaf of a crocus. The blooms themselves wouldn't come out for another week or two. There'd be no crocuses for us this Easter.

I wondered how long it would take for peace to bloom again. It had been a year since our involvement in the Great War had begun; despite everyone's efforts to win the fight and bring our boys home again, we were still stuck in what seemed like the same spot as last year. Would this war go on forever?

The only happy, blooming thing I saw around me was the love between Lucy and Will. I wished that made *me* happy too.

23

Pop surprised the whole family on Easter Sunday. He ventured off to Charlotte's flower shop up the street and bought each of us a flower to wear to church. Mine was a gardenia—the first real corsage I'd ever had. I couldn't stop admiring it—the velvety ivory petals and glossy satin leaves—and the aroma! It reminded me of something I cannot name, a soft, warm place I don't remember. Haunting, delicate, mine.

Oh, dear, I'm beginning to remind myself of Edna St. Vincent Millay! Except I am no poet. Maybe I am—or will be. I haven't really tried it yet.

This Easter, Mom finally got to sing the lovely solo she hadn't had a chance to perform last year, "I Know That My Redeemer Liveth." It was wonderful. The congregation sang the classic Easter hymns, with those of us who could read music providing harmony. As usual, I was pretty much oblivious to the rest of the show—the sermon and such.

Just before the end of the service, Mr. Warner strode down the aisle to the pew where we were sitting with Lucy and Will and announced their engagement to the entire congregation. There seemed to be plenty of folks who had not yet heard the news. A hubbub ensued.

"Those of you who wish to greet the happy young couple may join them in the social hall after the service. Refreshments will be served."

The whole congregation crowded into the social hall after church. Lucy and Will were instantly surrounded by a mob of well-wishers. A group of ladies gathered around Mom to learn all the details. Ida and the children who had gathered around her sat by one of the stained glass windows, which touched them all with its lovely blue and amber light. I stood with Pop next to the refreshment table, quietly devouring Mrs. Warner's chocolate cookies while Pop chatted with Mr. Muller.

"You say that your young man Fox comes from down by Cooperstown? I wonder if he's related to the J. W. Fox Silo Company?"

"Indeed he is! J. W. Fox was his father."

"Your girl is marrying a good man, then. And well-off too! Every farm for a hundred miles around has a Fox silo."

Pop smiled and nodded.

Mr. Muller went on. "Those Fox silos are a darn fine product! I bought mine twenty-three years ago and it's still as sound as the day it was built. I'm thinking of getting a second one now that I've increased the size of my herd."

As they launched into a debate about the virtues of Jersey versus Holstein cows, I excused myself and wandered in Ida's direction. As I approached, she glanced up at the clock on the wall, then rose from her chair to join me.

"I must go home now and prepare dinner for the family," she told the children who surrounded her.

"But the story!" said one girl. "You haven't finished the story!"

Ida chuckled quietly. "I haven't finished making it up! Why don't you children put your heads together and come up with an ending that *you* like? I'm dying to hear how the story comes out myself!" We left as the children eagerly began their discussion.

"You sure are a good teacher, Ida," I said. "Those children are ready to create their own ending to the story."

"That would be *surely*, Eleanor. And you, for your part, are a fine young student. I hope you extend your reach beyond Foersterville one day."

"But where?"

"I'd like to know how that comes out myself!"

Dinner was a bit rushed. That was partly because Will had to leave on the 4:30 train, but it was mostly to make sure John and I didn't miss the moments when the midafternoon sun lit up the back porch. It was the perfect setting for Will and Lucy's engagement photographs—especially since Mom had borrowed a couple of potted palms from church to dress up the scene for the pictures.

The perfect light arrived just as dinner was ending. Postponing dessert, we all trooped out to the porch to take the pictures. Mom brought the flower arrangement from the dining room buffet, all wrapped up and tied with a ribbon, for Lucy to hold as if it were a wedding bouquet. Of course it leaked water all over Lucy's dress. But we had a good laugh over it, then made sure that she posed to conceal the drip spots. John and I took pictures of Lucy and Will, then the two of them with Mom and Pop, then some with the whole family, including Ida and me. (For the family pictures, Mom insisted on leaving a gap where Francis should have been.) Just as we were finishing, Doc and Cora Baker stopped by the house on their way home from a walk with baby Vivian.

"It's a shame that you can't get one photograph with *all* of you," said Cora. "John, if you show me how to work that thing, I'll be glad to take one of the whole family." With a lot of encouragement from the rest of us, John agreed to get in *front* of the camera for a change while Cora took the picture.

Then it was time to go back inside for dessert. At Mom's insistence, the Bakers joined us—not for the coconut cream pie, Doc said, since they'd already eaten at home, but to meet Will and chat with him and Lucy for a bit.

The four of them sat in the parlor for half an hour and seemed to be getting on very well. Meanwhile, Vivian kept us busy in the dining room. Evidently she thought that the coconut pie was just fine; it took us some time to wipe it off her face, her dress, her hair, and even her shoes before turning her back to her parents' care, only a little the worse for wear. Vivian is a handful, but a sweet one.

It was time for Will to leave. After gathering his things, he bid us all a quick farewell before he and Lucy hurried off to the station for their longer goodbye.

I managed my part in this weekend pretty well, I thought. *Next time, I don't know. Namanamanama.*

24

Near the end of June, just two days before Lucy's graduation, we heard from Francis for the first time in several months, another penciled scrawl on paper torn from a tiny notebook:

Dear Mom and Pop,

I'm sorry I couldn't tell you before today, but here we are Over There. The French are delighted to see us "Doughboys," and we've been "feted," as they say, ever since we got here. I love these French people! Unfortunately, I can't tell you where we are or where we are going. Please trust that we are safely arrived and doing well.

I hope this gets to you before Lucy's graduation. Please tell her how proud I am to be her brother and how sorry I am to be missing her Big Event.

Your loyal son,

"François"

PS—Even in the middle of war, you see some mighty fine little pastries around here. "Petit fours," they call them. You'd love 'em, Ellie!

What a jolly message, I thought. Then I looked over at Mom, who didn't look jolly at all. She was wincing as if in pain. After a few seconds, she appeared to try to distract herself by drawing our attention away from the letter to Lucy's graduation and another visit from Will.

Graduation weekend was a real test of my newly mellow state. I must say I passed it with flying colors.

Will arrived the day before the ceremony. Right after supper that evening, in front of all of us, he presented Lucy with an engagement ring that held the biggest diamond I'd ever seen. It had been his mother's, he said.

Lucy glowed with joy, more beautiful than ever, as she accepted it. "You've told me how much your mother meant to you, Will," she said as he knelt before her, "and I love the thought of the woman who created such a son as you. I'm honored to wear her ring. I hope I earn the honor. I love you, Will."

They embraced each other first, and then the rest of the family. We all cried, even Pop. I wasn't crying from sadness, exactly, but I suppose more from relief. Will had made us his own family. Ida had been right when she said that he loved us all, and now we all loved him as much as I did . . . Will is ours.

That feeling lasted all the way through graduation day, when I helped Lucy into her frilly white graduation dress. The ritual made me think quite calmly about what it would be like to send the two of them down the aisle sometime in the future, when the war was over.

This time, though, there were twenty-five girls in white going down the aisles of the high school auditorium, along with sixteen boys in their Sunday best. They marched in two by two, except for Lucy. She was the only one who walked alone. She shone.

Lucy's awards that day were not of the academic kind. She won Most Popular, Most Helpful, and Most Enthusiastic. I was proud of my sister, and I wished I had some of her strong points. I wished I were more like her.

Reid was valedictorian. He looked quite respectable, almost distinguished, in the suit that John had lent him—even though it was a little tight across the shoulders, I noticed as he rose at the end of the program to give his speech.

Most of his speech was what you might expect from Reid, heavily salted with lines from his Latin heroes Caesar, Cicero, and Virgil. But then I began to see that he'd chosen his borrowed lines carefully; they reflected the dangers of the wartime world he and his classmates were graduating into, and the painful decisions many of them would have to make. He was wishing them the courage to make those decisions wisely, no matter how painful they might be. He made me wonder how much thought my dear old brother Francis had given to his decision to join the army and go off to war.

Reid ended by thanking the people who had helped him through high school. He mentioned his parents, who had supported his coming down to Foersterville even though it meant more work for them on the farm; John, who gave him a place to stay and helped him start a little farm of his own; his landlord Mr. Muller, Johnnie the grocer, Thelma the librarian—and his fast friend Lucy Foerster, whose belief in him helped him keep going in the most challenging moments.

Even Mom was impressed by Reid's speech: "That was quite a civilized performance by young Mr. Shoemaker. I would not have expected it of him."

I'm not sure whether Mom was moved to soften her opinion because Reid had appreciated her brother and daughter so publicly or because Lucy was firmly attached to Will, making her safe at last from Reid's "clutches," as she would put it.

Lucy and Will spent all day Saturday rowing the little pram up the river as far as they could go and then sailing back down again. A towel stretched between the oars was their sail, they said. By the time they got back, they had set their wedding date: the second Saturday after the end of the war.

They announced this decision over supper, and a lot more as well.

"We want to have a small, simple wedding, in keeping with the times, but *elegant* too," Lucy said. Mom didn't seem to warm to the "small, simple" part, but she perked up when Lucy mentioned "elegant." Pop's face, on the other hand, appeared to reflect the exact opposite view. Lucy and Will seemed to have hit upon a fine compromise between the fancy and the frugal. There was more to come.

"We considered having the wedding and the reception at church," said Will, "but then we thought that your beautiful home has such a long history as the setting for ceremonies like this that you might be willing to revive that tradition for us. It could be in the yard if the weather is clement, or in the parlor if not."

Pop jumped in. "Yes, Will, I well remember the many weddings we had here when my father still ran the Foerster Inn. When I was a young boy, one couple held their wedding and reception on the back lawn, and at the end, they were ferried down the river in a real Venetian gondola to catch the train for their honeymoon."

"Oh, Pop! I never *heard* that story!" said Lucy. "I promise, though, that I won't insist on a gondola for *our* escape!

"One more thing. No, *three*. If Francis is back in time, Will would like him to serve as best man—"

Will interrupted. "It was my good friend Francis who brought me to Foersterville in the first place and introduced me to the wonderful family I now think of as mine too."

"Two," Lucy went on. "Eleanor, would you be willing to serve as my maid of honor?"

"Wow! Of course I would!" I wasn't entirely clear on what a maid of honor does, but I knew I could figure that out later.

"And three. Ida, would you be willing to fashion our dresses for us?"

Ida nodded. "It will be a pleasure, my dear."

So everything was settled, at least as far as the wedding was concerned. But when would this damned war ever end?

25

Mom had been in good humor for Lucy's graduation and Will's visit, but soon afterward, she surprised us all with an eruption over dinner. The family had been talking about Francis's cheerful letter from France and wondering what he was doing today. All of a sudden, Mom stunned us with an outburst.

"I *thought* I had raised my only son to be *civil*! But *see* how he neglects his own family! We have had but half a dozen letters from him since he left us over a year ago."

Pop came to Francis's defense: "Keep in mind, Lily, that a soldier's life is hard. It leaves him little time to write. And there is much that the army doesn't permit him to say. Francis does as best he can, I'm sure."

Then, to my surprise, Mom hastily left the table and fled upstairs. I heard a door slam, then something between a moan and a scream. Pop went running up after her, leaving the rest of us to wonder what had just transpired. Lucy and I gaped at each other. We'd never seen her do that before, not even for our rudest behavior. Mom always keeps herself under control, even when she's annoyed at us.

Ida was the first to speak. "I suspect that your mother is more worried about Francis's well-being than she is angry at him, or at your father. It is hard for all of us to tolerate the uncertainty, but I would guess that is especially true for her. She is Francis's mother, after all."

Almost before Ida had finished speaking, we heard more sounds from upstairs: raised voices, a half-heard "Why do you *always* . . ." We three got up to clear and wash the dishes—but also to give Mom and Pop a bit more privacy. When our cleanup job was done, Ida, Lucy, and I embraced one another in the kitchen. It was not just Mom who worried about Francis; it was all of us. We needed each other to get through this time.

How could I help Mom? I wondered about that when I settled down in my little room that night. I couldn't tell her that everything would be okay. Maybe it *wouldn't* be okay. She was too smart to fall for empty reassurance. Maybe the best I could do was to keep quiet, try not to do anything that would upset her, and let Lucy cheer her up. The one bit of pleasure in her life these days was her delight in anticipating Lucy's wedding. I'd try not to distract her from that.

It seemed that Pop had the same idea. At the supper table one night soon after the outburst, he had a proposal:

"Lucy, I've been thinking. I know that Will is eager for you to visit him out in Oswego. This would be a good time to go. They say that Lake Ontario is beautiful at this time of year."

"She mustn't go without a chaperone!" said Mom.

"Yes, Lily, I've thought of that too. I speak for myself, but I think we could manage without you for a few days. I should miss you, of course, but would probably survive with the help of Eleanor and Ida."

"Oh, Pop! *Thank* you!" Lucy gushed. "I've been *longing* to see him in his own haunts. Will you go with me, Mom?"

She hesitated for a moment. "I shouldn't take the time away from my Red Cross projects—nor from my family."

"Will says there's a lot to see out there—the lake, of course, and the port on the lake, and a fine waterfall nearby. He tells me it's easy to get there by train from Syracuse and that there's a nice, clean hotel where we can stay without spending too much money."

"It sounds as if you and Will—and your father—have been plotting this outing for some time!" Mom frowned with mock disapproval.

"You have been working so hard on managing your Red Cross volunteers, Lily, that I thought it was time for you to have a bit of a vacation. The other ladies know by now how to carry on without you. For a little while, at least. The rest of us—Eleanor, Ida, and I—will do fine also, as long as you don't stay away from us for too long."

"I suppose I could manage it. For a few days. As long as we return promptly. I've never been to Lake Ontario. I should like to see it."

"You and Lucy will be the first in our family to venture that far west," Ida pointed out. "Please give us a full report when you get back!"

So it was decided.

It took a few days and a few telegrams to make the arrangements, but soon the two of them were off on their adventure.

They hadn't been gone but an hour when the mailman arrived with a new letter from Francis. Pop read it to us at the dinner table that day.

July 1, 1918

My Dear Family,

I meant to write you last Sunday, but one never knows what is coming next in the army. I had just settled down to compose my letter when I got called in on a detail to wash wagons and then give them a fine coat of oil as soon as they were dry. That night, I got called on duty once more, but this time it was a mistake since I'd already put in my time for the day. I volunteered to do it anyway, so at least I'd be excused from the _next_ *guard duty.*

It did surprise me to get shipped out here with so little notice. I had been hoping to get home for a visit at least once before I left, and several of my Foersterville friends had intended to come up to camp to see me. I kind of wish we'd had the chance.

Yes, I know I was eager to come here to fight, but a fellow can have two wishes at the same time, can't he?

With love,

Pte. Francis

PS—Ellie, I've learned a couple of silly French rounds that we'd have fun singing together. Can't wait to teach them to you!

PSS—I still haven't heard from Bess. Does she even remember me?

"Hmm." Ida looked pensive. "Bess Welk? From across the river?"

"Yes, Ida," I responded. "Francis has a soft spot for her."

"And she for him, I believe," said Ida. "In the past, I have often seen her walk by the house on some errand or other. But I can't say as she's been past here all this spring and summer—ever since I started sitting out on the front porch again. That could, of course, be because Francis is not here to see her. Or it may be that Bess is not here either."

"I have a meeting with her father tomorrow morning," said Pop. "I'll ask him then."

The next day at dinner, Pop had news. "Ida, you're a wonder! You seem to figure things out before anyone tells you," he said.

"Bob Welk told me that Bess went off to visit her cousins down near Binghamton last September. She'd intended to stay and help with the harvest, then be home for the holidays. But then, in December, she married an older man down there, a widower with a fine farm and three young children. Now they have one more baby—Bob's first granddaughter. A girl they call *Frannie*."

You could hear a pin drop around the table. Finally, Ida broke the silence: "It's probably best that Francis not know of this development just yet. The last thing he needs right now is a distraction from his dangerous work."

"I regret to say this, Ida, but I *did* tell Bob that Francis would like to hear from her, and I *did* give him our boy's address. That was before I knew about the marriage—or the child."

"I very much doubt that *she* will try to be in touch with him," said Ida. "My guess is that she hasn't the courage to tell him. But it's best that he not hear about this from any of us either, at least not until after he is safely home."

"I could not agree more," Pop replied. "Francis must not be distracted from his dangerous work."

"How about Mom and Lucy, Pop?" I asked. "Should we tell them when they get back?"

"I'd prefer it if we three could keep this news among ourselves and not talk to anyone about it—even Lily and your sister. I will let them know when it's the right time. Can you promise to keep the secret?"

"Yes, Pop. I promise not to talk about it with anyone but you—and Ida."

PART FIVE
PLAGUE

26

Lucy and Mom got home on the last Tuesday of July. Evidently they'd had a grand time. Mom was more relaxed and cheerful than I had seen her in months; Lucy, of course, was on top of the world. They also brought a pile of gifts for all of us—almost like a little summertime Christmas!

They brought saltwater taffy for everyone. Why it's called *saltwater* taffy is beyond me; everybody knows that Lake Ontario is a freshwater lake. (Everybody who got past the seventh grade, at least.) But the taffy tasted good, whatever it's called. For Ida, there was a souvenir plate showing the old lighthouse at Oswego; for me, a dainty silver spoon with a lake scene etched in the bowl; and for Pop, a handsome framed photograph of grain ships docked at the port. (Some of his grain, he says, comes from out West by way of the Great Lakes. I hadn't realized that—I always thought it all came from farmers right here in the valley.)

Over supper that night, they regaled us with stories of their travels from the hills of Iroquois County to the flatlands south of Lake Ontario. They'd seen grain and hay barges making their way along the Barge Canal, which runs next to the railroad. They saw orchards and vineyards replace the pastures and cornfields of our region as they traveled west. A stop at Syracuse, then a short train ride north to Oswego.

And then they delivered themselves to Will. He charmed them both.

"The best part of all was on Saturday!" Lucy announced. "Will rented an odd boat that runs like a bicycle, with *pedals* instead of oars or paddles. Will took Mom and me all around the harbor on this little vessel. We saw the old fort at the entrance to the harbor and all the ships at the docks inside. Then he took us back to a lovely luncheon at our hotel."

"Will was a gracious host," said Mom. "It's clear that he has had a proper upbringing. He's a fine young man."

"And he's really strong!" Lucy added, smiling contentedly.

The next letter from Francis arrived the following day, Wednesday, just before dinner. As soon as we sat down at the table, Pop picked up the knife at his place setting and carefully slit the envelope open. The little notebook pages slipped out onto his plate. He gathered them up and read the letter aloud to all of us:

July 14

Dear Mom and Pop,

Since July 1, we have been pretty busy. Our Company got a rest for ten days after being on the quiet front. Then we were sent north.

On the way, we came through what used to be a forest before it was torn to splinters by a major battle back in 1915. Some of the ragged trunks were ten feet high; some were but two. The ground was full of large and small holes, also trenches going every which way. Now the ferns and brush have grown over it, hiding many of the horrors of the field and making it even harder to traverse. The ground is rather rolling, but at one place we had to go over a very steep hill that had certainly received more than its share of artillery fire. We had to haul our gear through all this ragged, torn-up land, and when going over the steep hill, we had to stay in the trenches whenever we could manage it.

Our squads were small then but now they're smaller.

Yours,

Francis

PS—As we trudged through that battlefield, I made a lucky find, an abandoned pistol (a Luger) that some German soldier must have left behind in the battle. I cleaned it up. It seems to be in fine shape, and it even has seven bullets in it. It'll be a nice souvenir of the war when I come home, and a little extra protection for me until then.

PSS—It would be a good idea to keep Ellie from seeing this. I don't want her to worry too much.

Too late.

Mom closed her eyes for a minute and seemed to be trying to maintain her calm. After a big sigh, she was the first of us to speak. "I regret, girls, that you have been exposed to Francis's horrifying descriptions of the war, which are not appropriate for the ears of young ladies."

"It's okay, Mom," Lucy responded. "Whether it's 'appropriate' or not, Eleanor and I need to know the truth as much as you do. Right, Ellie?"

I nodded. I *think* she's right, but I wish I didn't have to know—and *live* with—this particular truth and all the dread that goes with it.

Mom softened. "You have a point, Lucy. I suppose I can't protect you girls forever. Much as I might wish to do so." She sighed again. "I suspected that Francis and his unit were about to move into danger when I read his last letter, about the special care they were giving to the wagons. But I did not expect them to be thrust into the midst of battle quite so soon. God help him."

"Yes," said Pop gravely. "He's beyond *our* help now."

Usually, we say grace before dinner only when we have company. Our grace is usually a cut-and-dried affair, just a little prayer that we all memorized years ago. Today was different. Pop asked us all to join hands around the table—something we *never* do.

Then he started praying: "Bless, O Lord, this food to our use. But *also* and *especially*, please bless our beloved son and brother, Francis. Lead him safely through this fearsome war and safely home to us, and on to a fine industrious future. We ask it in *Your* Son's name, Amen."

Then we all squeezed hands around the table before going on to an unusually somber meal together.

Just three days later, on August 1, we got our worst blow yet in this ugly war. The telegram said only that Private Francis Foerster had been seriously wounded in battle. It came from the War Department, cut-and-dried and free of any detail whatsoever.

Seriously wounded.

We heard nothing more from the War Department and nothing from Francis for a whole month. The wait was endless. Not one of us dared speak of it during that time, but of course not one of us stopped thinking and wondering and dreading what we might hear.

One day during that long wait, Mom sent me off to Johnnie's store for some groceries. On the way home, I encountered Reid as he headed up Verona Street with a delivery of produce.

"Hey there, kiddo! You're looking pretty morose. Are you dreading the start of school *already*? It's still a few weeks away."

"Reid! I didn't see you coming," I told him, thinking quickly to avoid letting him know what was really on my mind. "Seeing you reminds me that I've decided to follow your example and read the *Aeneid* in English before going back to study it in Latin this fall. You persuaded me that learning about a school subject in advance is not the same as cheating. Do you still have your copy of the—is it *Dryden*—translation?"

"Most assuredly so! I see it every morning when I wake up in my little shack."

"May I borrow it from you?"

"Of course you may—as long as you give it back to me when you're done. I have plenty of other books that can keep me busy. But the Dryden is a special favorite of mine!"

We agreed that he would bring it by the next time he made a delivery to Johnnie.

I'd need to get started on it right away to make any headway before going back to school. Maybe reading this old translation of an even older Latin saga would help distract me—for a while—from the only thing that *really* mattered to me now.

27

Dryden was such heavy going! It was *poetry*, and dense, old-fashioned poetry at that. I'd be lucky to make it through Book One before school started. This translation *couldn't* be any more comprehensible than the original Latin. And all this time, I'd thought the *Aeneid* was a love story, but it looked like a *war* story with a little love mixed in.

I guess you could say the same about my family these days—war and love all mixed together. I'd like just plain love a whole lot better.

Finally, on the first day of school, came the letter we'd all been waiting for. Francis was alive—and whole! The undated letter, written on real stationery this time, was lying open on the dining room table when I got home.

My Dear Family,

I am in Paris, getting ready to return to the front after being wounded last month. This is what happened.

We were just approaching our destination at the battlefield when we were attacked. I think I was gaping at the sight of men and horses flying through the air and the sound of all hell breaking loose when I was hit by flying debris—or more likely, a bullet. It got me on one cheek and went straight through my wide-open mouth and out the other side. The hit could have easily killed me or destroyed my face, but I was lucky. All I have to show for it is a pair of dimples that the nurses here tell me are "très adorables."

The YMCA man is giving the boys a talk. He says we are all going to be better men when we get back and that the States are going to be better, too, but he points out that there is one danger after every war, that many soldiers become tramps when they get home. It made the boys all laugh, for we all think that is what we've been getting the most training in.

Your own
Francis

PS—I think the war is nearly over. Things are getting warm. I know it. I'll be busy, so don't be surprised if I'm silent for a while.

I read his letter two or three times over before heading out to the kitchen, where Ida was finishing up her canning for the day.

We talked about Francis's letter as I tested a fair sample of her grape jelly while it was still warm, then helped her stow the jars in the cellar, clean up the kitchen, and prepare supper for the family. "Francis's letter is jollier than I expected," I told her.

"Perhaps a little too much so," said Ida. "I fear that he is so taken by the attractions of Paris that it will be hard for him to don his boots and go back out into the field."

"I'd be scared to go back after having such a close call."

"That's quite a reasonable response, Eleanor. But a soldier *has* to go back even though he is scared half to death. As unwise as he may have been to do so, your brother made his commitment. The soldier is honor bound to stand by it."

At supper, Pop read Francis's letter aloud for us all to hear. We talked about how relieved we all are that Francis is now safe, but nobody mentioned the future. Ida held her tongue, and I followed her example.

Homework was rather easy tonight. It always is on the first day of school. The teachers want to warm us up a bit, I think, before the real work begins.

The hardest assignment for me was Latin. Mrs. Brown had told us in class about the *Iliad* and the *Odyssey*, the Greek epics that had inspired Virgil and were already ancient by the time he came along. She read us the part of the *Iliad* where Aeneas escapes the burning city of Troy while carrying his aged father on his back. The *Aeneid*, she said, continues his story after that.

Then she gave us our assignment to translate just the first sentence of the poem. "Don't worry," she told us, "whether your translation sounds like poetry. Just write down what you think Virgil is telling us."

Easier said than done. I struggled over the meaning—the *plain* meaning, not the fancy poetic expression of it. Even the first three words, *Arma virumque cano*, gave me a great deal of trouble. I finally settled on this: "My poem is about war, and about a soldier." I'm rather proud of that. I think its meaning is a lot clearer than "Arms and the man I sing," Dryden's attempt at expressing the same idea in English. But then, he was a poet—and so, I suspect, dedicated to obfuscation.

I got to bed rather early. Sometime in the night, I awoke from a nightmare, terrified. Francis was in it. I was standing at the edge of a wide, wide river, waving to him on the other side as he waved back at me. I became aware of some dreadful monster coming up behind him—a dragon, or maybe a train. I tried to shout a warning, but no sound came from my mouth. I tried warning him with gestures, but he remained oblivious to the danger. He was about to be smashed when I woke, my mouth wide open as if to scream.

I rushed across the hall to Lucy's room and climbed up onto the bed with her. I needed her to hold me. She came out of her own dreams enough to take me in her arms, embracing me until my monster faded. Then we both slept again. We woke up early and talked for a while before getting up.

"What gave you the bad dream last night, Ellie?"

"Francis's letter, I think. I'm so afraid for him! He's been wounded once already, and yet here he is going right back into battle. I worry that he'll be hurt worse next time, and all of us will have to stand helplessly by when it happens."

"Oh, Eleanor, you missed the most important part of the letter—except for the fact that Francis is well, of course. He knows that the war will end soon. That means Francis will be home with us again, and Will and I will be free to marry at last. Life will go on as before, only better!"

I hope so.

28

Doc and Cora and little Vivian were with us for supper in mid-September when Lucy brought Will's most recent letter to the table. She doesn't usually let us know what's in her letters from Will, I guess because they must be too mushy for her to want to show around. But she did read this one to us, at least in part—maybe because Doc was there:

> *In the past few weeks, quite a few soldiers have been sent here to Fort Ontario with a new disease, the "Spanish influenza." We have been so busy caring for these patients that we have stopped receiving new cases from outside our hospital. Some of these boys get over the flu in a few days, but some are very ill.*
>
> *Don't worry about me, dear Lucy. The staff have been taking the utmost care to keep from coming down with this disease ourselves. To work in the ward, we prepare as carefully as if we were getting ready to perform surgery.*

After hearing this, Doc looked concerned. "The Spanish flu has popped up in a lot of places, I've heard, especially in and around military bases. I'm hoping that here in Iroquois County, we will be protected by our relative isolation. I wish I could promise that."

I wish he could have too. The flu showed up within days. The telegrapher at the train station was the first to get it. Some people thought he'd picked it up from a passenger who got off the train from Albany, though it was never clear just which passenger it might have been.

This outbreak led the school district to decide that as a safety precaution, we and our teachers had to wear gauze masks in classrooms. The new rule came soon after the start of the fall term, just as John was preparing to take our yearbook photographs. I didn't help him set up the pictures, but I did have to help sort out who was who in each of the high school classes. It's not easy when everyone's in disguise.

Here in Foersterville, we wore our masks in church, on the street, and inside all the stores along Iroquois—except for the ones that wouldn't even let us enter; they made us place our orders outside and wait for delivery at the shop door.

And still, some people got sick: Mr. Lloyd, the stationer, got it early. (He picked up the Albany paper at the station every day, so the theory was that he had contracted it from the telegrapher.) It was lucky that he didn't get sick until a few weeks after school started; he could have passed it on to students who bought their supplies from him, and from them to the whole school.

At first, everyone was okay at our house.

But then Mom brought it home.

She came down with the flu in late September and retired to her room to wait it out. Pop moved into Francis's room across the hall for the duration.

We never did figure out where Mom got it. She had so many connections through church and the Red Cross and ladies' clubs that we couldn't sort out where her infection sprang from. Fortunately, it was not too serious, though it did make her a bit crankier than usual.

Mom would not let anyone in our family take care of her. "I will *not* allow my loved ones to be exposed to this disease, which is unpleasant at the least and lethal at the worst!" Pop hired Annie MacNeil, a sweet old lady who has made it her life's work to tend to invalids and children.

Mom was not pleased with Annie Mac's ministrations. She fired her after two days. "That woman has no common sense whatsoever! She thought she was helping me pass the time by reading articles from the newspaper—but the stories that interested her were the obituaries of local people who have *died* of influenza. The very *idea*!"

Pop had to find another nurse. Cora volunteered, and Lucy agreed to take care of little Vivian while Cora nursed Mom. That meant we had to move all the bric-a-brac from the parlor and dining room and store it away where Vivian couldn't see it. At just two, Vivian is full of curiosity. She loves to walk and run and climb and reach for anything that catches her eye. If she could have reached them, she would have made fast work of Mom's collection of delicate porcelain figurines.

Mom seemed to be doing well under Cora's care. Each day when I entered the front hall after school, I could hear them chatting and laughing behind her closed bedroom door upstairs. Doc checked on her every day, and he agreed with Cora that Mom was doing very well. Every time Doc visited, he checked Cora and the rest of us, too, to make sure we had no symptoms.

Doc finally set Mom free from her sickroom just ten days after she came down with the flu. Her symptoms were gone; by then, she was even strong enough to help Cora disinfect the room before making her way down to the parlor to settle into the big chair by the front window. It took her most of that day and the next to gather her strength before venturing farther afield. The family was allowed to visit with her, but only one or two of us at a time. Finally, on Sunday, Pop moved back into the bedroom with her, and things returned to a semblance of normal.

Up to a point. The next afternoon, on the last day of September, my homeroom teacher, Miss Cole, read an announcement from the school superintendent: "The local intensification of the influenza epidemic requires that the Iroquois Valley School District close all schools from the end of the day today until the epidemic abates. We anticipate reopening on Monday morning, November 4. Should there be any change in that plan, you and your family will be notified via US Mail."

A whole month away from school? This would be like a little summer vacation! You could feel the excitement rise among us. Miss Cole quickly put a lid on that.

"You need to gather all of your textbooks and take them home with you today. Each of your subject-matter teachers has prepared an outline of the material that you are required to cover by the time school is expected to resume. You must take on the responsibility to learn this material well enough to demonstrate proficiency upon your return. Stay in your seats until I call each of you to give you your assignment. As soon as you receive the assignment, you will be dismissed. Be prudent and take good care of yourselves during this period. I hope to see you all when this ordeal is over."

Then, one by one, we walked up to her desk at the front of the room, lugging our books and supplies. She handed each of us a single sheet of paper, a list of assignments from all our subject-matter teachers. She gave each of us a few words of encouragement and farewell, and then we made our way home for the duration.

As she handed me the assignment sheet, Miss Cole said, "If you race through these assignments, Eleanor, there is nothing to prevent you from exploring beyond them, you know. Keep yourself busy, and keep yourself well."

I must say that at first glimpse, I was impressed by how few lines the assignments took up on the page. *This'll be easy*, I thought. But then I started looking at the mass of details hidden by the simple words of the assignments: chapter after chapter of reading in English, history, algebra, Latin, and physics, with exercise after exercise in each chapter. It might not have seemed so hard if the work had been issued one day at a time, but served up all at once, it was daunting!

Rosie was waiting for me when I left the building. I never see her in classes because she's a year behind me in school. We've been best friends since grade school. When I saw Rosie, I wanted to hug her. It might be a whole month before we got to see each other again. We lugged our overwhelming loads of books down Iroquois to my house and dropped off my share on the front porch. Then I took part of her load and we continued up Verona Street to Rosie's house. Along the way, we wondered how we could ever complete our gigantic assignments in just one month.

Rosie had a practical idea. "I looked at a calendar," she said. "Beginning tomorrow, we have thirty-four days, including Saturdays and Sundays, to do our homework. What if we just divide our assignments into thirty-four parts? Then at least we'll know how much we have to finish each day to get it all done in time."

"You sound like Mom! She tells me that when you have a big task to do, like learning to sing a whole oratorio, you have to 'divide and conquer.' You can't do it all at once, and you can't put it off while waiting for inspiration to strike. Now I begin to see what she means."

By the time we arrived at Rosie's house, we were just getting started on our grand homework plan. We decided that we'd keep on talking while she walked *me* home. Along the way, we agreed on some other ground rules: to study every subject each day so we wouldn't get rusty in any of them, to ask friends and family for tutoring help, and to send each other a progress report every week.

We were still so reluctant to part that I walked Rosie home *again*. This time we talked about something far more important—to her, at least.

"What do you think of Harold?" she ventured.

"Harold?" I wondered which one of the three or four Harolds at our school she was referring to.

"Yes, Harold Holtzman," she said softly.

"Oh, him. He's in a couple of classes with me. He seems to do okay." I was a little puzzled by her question.

"I mean, what do you *think* of him? Nice, charming, handsome? What do you *think*?"

Oh, *that* kind of think. "Can't say that I've ever studied him."

To the extent that I'd studied him, I thought he was rather . . . callow. But of course I wouldn't tell Rosie that. Anyway, I didn't suppose my opinion of Harold mattered much to her. She wanted to tell me what *she* thought of him. My job was to listen.

"Is he a friend of yours?"

"Not yet. But I want to make him one. I think he's the most attractive boy in the whole school—tall, smart, witty . . . and an athlete! And I think he noticed me the other day in the lunchroom. I smiled, and he smiled back."

"I never saw him pay even that much attention to a girl. Sounds like you're breaking new ground! Say, the spring ball is coming up in March—assuming life is back to normal by then. Maybe he'll invite you."

"You read my mind, Ellie. How did you know that was my goal?"

“I don’t know. Guess I was in the same boat once.” All of a sudden, I felt incredibly old.

Fortunately for me, Rosie didn’t even seem to notice my comment—or the sigh that followed.

This time, I dropped Rosie off at her house and then took a shortcut back to our place. By the time I arrived, the family was just sitting down to supper. I ran upstairs to put my books away and wash up, then tore back down and tried to make a quiet, dignified entry. Not very successfully, it seems.

“Where in the world have you been all this time, Eleanor?” Mom inquired coolly. I remembered that tone from the day Francis disappeared. She was not happy.

I apologized, then reported the day’s momentous news about school’s closing. Finally, I told the family about the homework plan Rosie and I had worked out during our extended walk home.

Mom was mollified. “You girls showed admirable initiative,” she said. “Your plan seems like a solid one. How do you plan to prepare for it tonight?”

I had been thinking that I would take the night off and get started in the morning. But Mom’s question made me realize that dividing all that work up in a reasonable way was a big task in itself; finding tutors and figuring out how to use their assistance, an even bigger one.

Right here at the supper table, we had a rich source of potential tutors. Why not ask them?

“I’ll start right now, Mom. Will you be my English tutor?”

She seemed a bit taken aback. “Why me?” she asked. “What do you anticipate my doing?”

“Well, Mom, I think you are a fine, clear writer. And there’s no one more careful with grammar and usage than you are. I think you'd be able to spot my mistakes and help me correct them." That seemed to satisfy her.

I went on: "It's not hand-holding that I need. I'll do each day's assignment myself and then turn it in to you. You can look it over and make corrections. If I don't understand—or agree with—your comments and corrections, we can meet."

"That sounds like a workable arrangement to me," said Mom. "Yes, I'll be your English tutor. Happily." Then, with a wink to Ida, she said, "I may have to consult with *my* teacher from time to time."

Lucy said she'd help me with algebra and physics, her two favorite courses last year. Pop volunteered for history. And Ida, the only real teacher among them, agreed to answer questions and resolve differences that we couldn't settle ourselves.

The only subject that nobody volunteered for was Latin. Lucy was adamant: "I took Virgil last year, hated it, and nearly flunked the course. I'll never make a tutor in Latin." Nobody else at the table could either, which put me in something of a pickle. As much as I enjoy it, Latin is *hard*. It was the one course in which I would really need a tutor.

I wondered if Reid would be willing.

29

The leaves of the elms along Verona Street were turning yellow, and across the river, a few maples in Mr. Muller's big sugar bush were beginning to glow red. It was early yet, but in a couple of weeks, the hills around Foersterville would be in their full fall glory. Autumn is our most beautiful season here—perhaps because it fades so quickly into the dullness of winter.

This morning I was still lounging around in bed, admiring the river view, when I spotted Reid trudging up Verona with a wheelbarrow full of pumpkins and winter squash—to sell at Johnnie's store, no doubt. I jumped up, threw on some clothes and my mask, and ran out to meet him so I could ask him to be my Latin tutor.

It took me a while to ask. Reid was working too hard with the wheelbarrow to talk much, and I was breathless from the rush to meet him, so I waited until his work was done to make my request. I felt awkward about running up to him out of nowhere to ask a big favor. I did try to lighten his load a bit, though, by lifting a couple of the smaller pumpkins out of the cart and carrying them up to his destination—Johnnie's delivery door in the alley behind the store. I waited there while he finished his business. Then I made my move.

"Um, did you know that school has been canceled until November because of the flu?"

"That's news to me. How do you plan to pass the time?"

"Homework!"

Enough chitchat. Now was the time to ask him. "I wonder," I said. "Do you have time to be my Latin tutor? Until we get back to school, I mean."

"Not if you just want me to do your homework for you."

"Oh, no! What I want is for you to look over my homework every few days to let me know what you think I need to fix and why. It might involve meeting somewhere once or twice a week."

"Well . . . I suppose I could manage that. I make deliveries here in town, and I have to come up here to buy the food I can't grow or catch."

"Do you know when you'll be back next time?"

"Saturday, I believe."

"Can we meet then? On the front porch if it's nice, or inside if it's raining." (I was hoping I could get Mom to go along with this plan.)

"We can give it a try."

"Oh, *thank* you, Reid! Here's the homework I've done so far. Will you look it over?"

Reid smiled. I hope he didn't think me overenthusiastic—I was just trying to get my work in order. "Okay, El. I'll see you Saturday."

Much to my relief, Mom did not disapprove of my inviting Reid into the house. At least, not very much. She recognized, I guess, that he's the only one any of us knows who could possibly serve as a Virgil tutor. "Just do not get too personal with this young man, dear, for your own good. He is not well-bred."

Even if he's not well-bred, he is the most serious Latin scholar in Foersterville, and that's why I wanted to work with him. Mom worries about her girls too much. No one could possibly see Reid as some sort of Lothario—except for Mom, of course.

Saturday was warm for October, so Reid and I sat on the porch to go over my first week's homework. I checked quickly through the pages. He'd made a few corrections, but not so many as I'd feared he would.

"You did a creditable job, kiddo. You're really learning your Latin—the grammar and vocabulary, at least. But you still have a ways to go to get the music of it. Your translation is rather flat-footed, El."

He went all the way back to my opening line: *My poem is about war, and a soldier.*

"You missed the cultural meaning of the very first verb, *cano,* 'I sing.' Back in Greek times, poets were singers. Great epics like the *Iliad* and the *Odyssey* were passed down orally for generations before anyone ever wrote them down. Virgil created his epic much later; instead of actually *singing* his work, he wrote it down for a literate audience. But his use of the verb *cano* would have reminded his readers of the olden days, the days when poets really did sing. It was important for setting the scene."

"So a metaphor is not always meant just to be obfuscatory, I guess."

Reid grinned broadly—that same crooked smile that used to strike me as diabolical. Now, it didn't alarm me at all.

"*Obfuscatory*, eh? That's a hell of a word, Eleanor. You must eat dictionaries every day for breakfast. But yes, in the hands of a good poet, a metaphor can add depth and beauty to a thought that might otherwise fall flat."

I must admit that he had a point.

Right after she got engaged, Lucy took on the job of picking up our daily mail at the post office. She couldn't bear waiting even a few minutes to read her letters from Will. I was just finishing my meeting with Reid on the front porch when she came running toward us down Iroquois. She looked agitated.

"Will has it!" she cried as she collapsed into one of the porch rockers. "He's a patient in his own hospital!" Then she started to cry.

I knelt next to her and held her until she started to compose herself. She handed me the letter.

Sweet Lucy,

I hope you and your dear family are well.

The fates seem to have decided I have been working too hard lately. I have come down with a fairly mild case of the "disease of the day" and am now in the infirmary to rest up. My comrades are taking excellent care of me. I should be ready to go again within a few days. Please don't worry about me. I am strong and fit, and I am getting the best of care.

Now I will sleep. My dreams will be of you, as always.

Your own

Will

Now I was crying right along with Lucy.

Reid took the situation in hand. "You girls need to be with your family," he said gently. He ushered us into the house and down the hall to the kitchen, where Mom and Ida were sitting at the table, chatting over tea.

Ida saw us first. "My land, girls! What *happened*?" She pulled up two more chairs and was about to bring a third when Reid shook his head. "Thank you, Miss Klaus, but you needn't bring a chair for me. This is a family matter." He nodded, then left quickly by the back door.

Mom's eyes followed him suspiciously. "Has that boy been *rude*?"

"No, Mom." I sighed. "He's been ever so thoughtful to both of us."

"It's Will," Lucy said through her tears. She handed the letter to Mom, who read it aloud to Ida.

Then Mom spoke. "Remember, girls, this is a disease you've seen before. For most people, it's no worse than a cold. I got over it quickly, and so did Henry Lloyd and Eli the telegrapher and almost everyone else who has contracted it here in Iroquois County. Will is young. He is likely to come through his bout with influenza without difficulty, just as I did."

I hoped so. Lucy sniffled, and Mom handed her a handkerchief.

Ida poured us some tea. She added her own bit of wisdom. "It will be hard for you, Lucy—indeed, for all of us who love him—to stay patient as we wait for further news from Will. He is far away, in the experienced hands of the army. There is nothing you or any of us can do except wait, and hope, and pray for his quick recovery. We must be patient."

"Just as we're learning to do with Francis," I thought. "We can't imagine what is happening to him, and there's no way we can help, so we just have to take a deep breath and wait. And wait some more." The thought made me cry again—this time, the quiet tears of helpless grief.

That's life on the home front. We *try* to make a difference, what with our knitting projects and bandage-making projects, our meatless Tuesdays and wheatless Wednesdays, our endless Liberty Bond drives. But in the end, our boys are all alone out there and we are helpless to save them from anything.

Later in the day, Doc Baker showed up at the back door. He refused Ida's offer to come in.

"I don't want to expose you unnecessarily," he said. "Cora has come down with it. At least it *looks* like the flu, though it still may turn out to be a bad cold."

Mom came in just as he was making his announcement. "In that case," she said, "Cora will need a nurse. I have already had influenza, and Cora has already shown me how to be a good nurse. I will be there as soon as I can pack my things."

"Thank you, Mrs. Foerster. Because I am so involved in treating other patients in the community, I couldn't take on those responsibilities myself. I came here to ask you that very favor. Cora takes great pleasure in your company. She asked for you."

Lucy offered to take on Vivian's care, but this Doc declined. "Thank you, Lucy, but Cora and I feel she needs to be at home with us. Annie Mac will tend to her until Cora gets better."

Mom gathered together her essentials, kissed us all farewell, and moved down the street to Doc and Cora's house for a few days, where she would stay until Cora recovered. We wouldn't see her again until Doc told us it was safe.

Meanwhile, Ida and Lucy took over the household management.

And I kept plugging away at my homework.

30

The next day we heard from Francis at last. Lucy picked his letter up at the post office, again while I was working with Reid on the front porch. She borrowed Reid's pocket knife to slit it open, then read it to us:

Dear Folks at Home,

I'm back in the hospital, recovering from another injury. I got shot. Actually, I shot myself. Accidentally. I was cleaning my trophy Luger when it went off and struck me in the calf of the leg. That was just before we began our big push at the end of September. I have healed pretty well and can now walk without too much of a limp. I should be ready to go back to my unit soon.

Write me.

Francis

PS—I didn't get back to Paris this time, but had to stay in a hospital near the front. It's like being in jail! The nurses are tough and bossy, but a little nicer than they were when I first arrived. They thought I might have hurt myself on purpose. Ha! There's no chance of that!

I'm glad she read it aloud. It wasn't the end of the world. Francis was alive. He would keep on living.

After Lucy went into the house, Reid made one of his characteristically acid remarks: "On the eve of battle? I wonder if it was intentional."

I gasped. "How can you *possibly* say that, Reid?" What I thought was, *My brother is a brave soldier, and you are a draft dodger!* But I didn't say it. Part of me knew that Reid is courageous, too, in his own way—but not the part that was outraged by what he said about my own Francis.

"Just a speculation," he replied calmly. "The timing *is* interesting."

It took a while for me to calm down, but eventually, we got back to our work with Virgil. Under Reid's tutelage, I'm getting pretty good at Latin. The *poetry*, even. Reid is a smart fellow, I have to admit—but unfortunately, he's also a smart aleck.

31

I came downstairs after a morning of studying in my room to find Lucy and Ida sitting together on the parlor settee. I guessed at first that they were doing fancywork together. Then I saw the tears.

"What is it?" I asked. "Is it Francis?"

"Not Francis," Lucy said through her tears. She held up a piece of paper—it looked like a telegram. I could see only part of it: *WE REGRET TO INFORM YOU . . .*

"Will. It's *Will.* He's gone," she told me flatly.

I dropped my books, pulled up a chair, and joined the grieving circle.

Then the doorbell rang. We pulled ourselves together as best we could, and Ida rose to open the door. It was the postman with a special-delivery letter for "Miss Lucy Foerster." Ida turned the thick envelope over to Lucy, who excused herself and hurried upstairs to read it in her bedroom.

She did not come downstairs again for dinner with the rest of us, so I took her a tray. She told me she needed the time to grieve alone. I kissed her and left.

Later that night, she asked me to sleep in the big bed with her. She let me read the letter. It was from Oscar, Will's best friend at the base, a fellow whom Lucy had met on her trip to Oswego. Just touching the letter was painful. I had to steel myself to read it.

Dear Miss Foerster,

Will passed away quietly today. I was with him. Not long before he let go, he asked me to send you the enclosed envelope and tell you that he treasures your love. I know this to be true because I have heard him speak many times of his deep affection for you and your family, the only real family he ever had. You and your folks must be devastated by his loss, as am I, who honored him as my closest friend and guide.

With my sincere condolences,

Pvt. Oscar Rains

Lucy's hand quivered a little as she handed me the other envelope, the one from Will himself. I was hesitant even to touch it. I had to brace myself to take it from her hand.

"Go ahead, Ellie. You can read it. He would have wanted you to."

So I gritted my teeth, slipped the note out of its envelope, and read:

Dearest Lucy,

Love of my life,

I have asked Oscar to send you this letter in the case of my death.

Even in death, I want you to know how deeply I cherish you and your love for me.

I want your beloved family to know, too, of my profound attachment to them all: lively, charming Francis; Eleanor the relentless explorer; your strong, protecting parents; and dear Ida, who embraces all of you.

If it is possible, I wish to be buried in the Foersterville cemetery, somewhere near the Foerster plot. I ask this because yours is the only real family I have ever known, and of course because I cannot bear to be separated by more than a few feet from my dearest love, Lucy.

Oh, my Lucy, I do so wish that we had had a chance for a life and a family together. It is not to be. I hope with my whole heart that you find a loving man with whom to share your life and children. I will bless them all.

Your own Will

What was there to say? We held each other and wept until we had no more tears, and then we fell into exhausted sleep.

Lucy was up and gone by the time I opened my eyes the next morning.

A lacy white veil hung from the bedpost, haunting the room like a ghost. Cora had worn it for her own wedding to Doc, and just last week, she had lent it to Lucy for hers. I got up, folded it carefully, and tucked it into one of the drawers of the big bureau we had brought over from my room across the hall. Why remind her so blatantly of her dreadful loss?

Looking around the room, I saw that it was heavy with other reminders too—the most recent of the pretty and useful things she had been given for her trousseau. I found places for most of the gifts in the bureau and tucked a few more onto a shelf in the closet.

Now only the big, beautiful marriage bed was left. It made all the rest of my tidying up seem pointless.

Oh Lucy, how can you go on?

It was late when I finally made my way downstairs. Ida was already gone. Pop should have left too—it was long past the time when he usually headed down to the mill. But he and Lucy were still sitting at the table, deep in conversation—or was it an argument? As

I tiptoed around the kitchen to collect some bread and cheese for breakfast, they carried on without even seeming to notice that I was there.

"I know you're upset, Lucy," Pop was saying quietly, "but look at the letter again. Will knew what was appropriate—he said *near* the family plot, not *in* it."

I could tell that Lucy was having a hard time staying calm. "But Pop! You told me yourself that he was like a second son to you."

"He was indeed, dear Lucy," Pop replied in a soothing voice.

"Then why *not* give him a place in the family plot?"

"Had you been married when we lost him, he surely would have had a place in our family plot. But as hard as it may be for you to consider today, you are still young enough to marry another fine young man, one who will deserve that honor in the future. Think how he would feel about your sleeping for all time between him and another man whom you never married."

Lucy paused before answering. She seemed to be fighting back a sob. I know *I* was.

"No, Pop! Never! I could never marry a man who didn't respect my love for Will—and his for me. I would *despise* such a man. Wouldn't you?"

"But it would be reckoned as very odd in Foersterville for a family to give space in the family plot to one who was related neither by blood nor marriage." Pop is a great believer in local traditions.

As upset as she was, Lucy seemed to sense an opening. She must have suspected that Pop was even more attached to his own family's traditions than to local customs. "What about Ida, Pop?" she pointed out. "There is a family space reserved for her, yet she's no relation either. She will be buried next to your uncle Charles, a man she loved but never got a chance to marry."

There was a long pause as Pop sighed and looked up at the ceiling. Then he looked back down at Lucy and said, "Yes, my girl, you do make a good point. Indeed, I remember as if it were yesterday when my father opened our home to her—and offered Ida her own space in the family plot. She seemed very grateful then and does to this day." He paused a moment. "And Foersterville did not raise an eyebrow, come to think of it.

"Yes," Pop added. "I suppose I should follow Father's precedent and do the same for Will. It seems that is what Father would have wanted. On Saturday afternoon, you and I shall visit the family plot and choose a grave site for him—and one for you beside him. We'll just have to make sure there is an open space on the other side of you, for—"

"Yes, Father!" Lucy interrupted. She jumped up and kissed him as if he were offering her a palace. A few minutes later, she was off to make funeral arrangements with Pastor Warner and Mr. Wilbur's funeral home.

That girl can move from despair to diligence faster than I could ever manage! I think it's making all those arrangements that is keeping her from falling to pieces. At least for now.

At dinner, the rest of us all agreed to spare Mom from hearing the news of Will until she returned from her work with Cora. We remembered how annoyed she had been at Annie Mac's tales of death when Mom herself was ill. Why would we expose her and Cora to the same distraction while Cora was recovering from her own case of influenza?

The next morning, Reid showed up on the doorstep. I had completely forgotten that he was coming; it was the first time since we had been working together that I had neglected to do my homework. This was just the kind of laziness he'd been expecting of me all along.

Would he decide I'm not worth the trouble? I was reluctant to go to the door. But where else to go?

"I have nothing to show you, Reid. I'm sorry to let you down."

"Sounds like you've let *yourself* down, kiddo. You've always been ready before. What happened this time?"

I struggled to keep my composure while I said it. "Will is . . . gone. Influenza. We found out two days ago."

He looked aghast. "Not Will! So young! Promising! How hard it must be for you all—especially *Lucy*—to lose him. I'll miss him too. It was hard not to love that fellow. I'll be glad to help if I can."

"It would help me just now if you could sit with me while I catch up on my homework."

"But you know, kiddo, that you've long since finished your assignment from Mrs. Brown. Indeed, you're within a day or two of finishing the whole course! Why not let yourself settle back for a few days while you grieve with your family?"

"I need that work to keep me from going crazy." What I didn't tell him was that I needed his company too. As long as he didn't start making wisecracks about my brother.

"Okay, then. Let's translate the last few stanzas together. Don't hesitate to stop if you need to."

I was glad for one thing, at least. Reid no longer saw me as a leech who wanted to suck his knowledge out of him and display it as my own. It was a small pleasure—but a pleasure.

We made it all the way through to the end of the poem. The end of the *Aeneid* is not soothing, as I'd hoped it would be. Aeneas kills yet another of his enemies. That's supposed to solve everything. I'd hoped for some calm and peace at the end, but the only peace comes from the deaths of all of Aeneas's foes. I wish there were *real* peace. And less death.

32

As we were finishing our breakfast on Friday morning, an eerie wraith appeared on our back porch, masked and dressed all in white. Lucy and I gasped in alarm, but Pop raced to the door.

"Sweetheart! What brings you here so suddenly?"

Of *course* it was Mom. She was still masked and in her nursing garb, out of breath after running here from the Bakers' house.

"Cora. Died. Just now." Her voice was dull, flat.

Pop reached out to embrace her.

"Do not *touch* me!" she cried out, recoiling. "I cannot allow my *family* to be exposed to this . . . hell!"

"Then how *can* I help you, Lily?"

"Follow me back. Sit on the porch while I go up to . . . *her.* Wait for Doc. He is on morning calls. Tell him. This is what you can do."

Without another word, Pop grabbed a coat from the hall and followed her down the steps.

Lucy had the presence of mind to telephone the mill and let them know he would be delayed in arriving at work.

Ida embraced both Lucy and me in a ritual that had become all too familiar—and *necessary*—of late. Then we sat back down at the breakfast table, not wanting to be without each other's company.

I loved Cora. The merry jingle of her shoes as she walked. Her mastery of all things practical: making bandages, driving an automobile. Her good humor. Her warm friendship. What would Doc and little Vivian ever do without her? And the rest of us too?

"Cora!" said Lucy. "She was such a live wire. I never expected it."

"Nor I!" said Ida. "The longer we live with this scourge, though, the more it seems that it singles out the young and strong. The more mature among us, like your mother, seem to skate by without serious consequences."

I thought about returning to school next Monday with all those strong young people, but I kept my fears to myself.

I thought of Mom. She loved Cora too. And Will. When she returned home, we couldn't keep Will's death to ourselves. How could she bear losing both of them? How could we all?

Pop returned at about two in the afternoon. He had a cold luncheon of leftovers before rushing off to the mill for the rest of the business day. Before he left, he asked us to take Mom a change of clothes; she would be coming home, bringing Vivian with her, as soon as they had bathed and dressed.

While I waited for their arrival, I ran up to the attic to sort through a big old trunk filled with outgrown toys from my generation of Foerster children, and from at least two generations of Foersters before us. I chose good, sturdy ones that I had loved—Pop's hardwood blocks, early favorites of mine; Francis's cast-iron fire truck, which I loved when I was Vivian's age; and Lucy's Alice in Wonderland doll, which she had always kept tidy and perfect before I tried to give her a chignon. Alice became severely disheveled after that episode. And good Lucy never complained.

I took these treasures down to my room to bring out if Vivian needed them.

About an hour before dinner, Mom rolled in, pulling a child's red wagon behind her. It held a couple of valises—Mom's clothing, I supposed. Perched on top was Vivian, whooping and giggling with glee at the adventure. She clutched the giant bear that I had won for her at the fair over a year ago. (It seemed like a century.) That bear had become her favorite toy. I could tell: The two blue button eyes were missing, along with one ear and most of the embroidered nose. She called it Cherry Bearie.

I'm glad I gave Vivian her own treasure.

Before retiring to her room for a short time alone, Mom told us that Doc would be joining us for dinner, perhaps for several days.

"I cannot imagine that he will want to suffer alone at home," she said. "Hence, I invited him to stay here for as long as he needs. Can you prepare Francis's room for Doc while I rest a bit?"

Ida, Lucy, and I worked together to ready the room. Sweeping the carpet, dusting, opening the windows to air the room out, making sure the windows were clean. Ida and I made up the bed. Meanwhile, Lucy gathered towels, made sure the washbasin was clean, and filled the pitcher with fresh water.

At one point, when Lucy was out of the room, Ida said to me, "Would you mind, Eleanor, taking little Vivian upstairs for a quiet supper while the rest of us are in the dining room? I believe that the adults need to say things that she is not ready to hear."

"Things? What things?"

"Your mother doesn't know yet . . . about Will."

Will.

I agreed to babysit for Vivian. But that wasn't the end of my thinking about the situation. On one hand, I was honored that Ida trusted me to take responsibility for Vivian's protection. On the other, I wondered if Ida was trying to keep *me* safe, too, from the evening's pain and grief. Had Vivian and I been relegated to the children's table? I must say that this thought raised my hackles. Am I such a baby that I needed to be protected from the sadness around me? Was I not grieving too?

It took me a while, sitting alone in my little room, to recover my balance.

Ida knows me, I thought. *She knows that I can live through profound pain because she has watched me do it. She doesn't think of me as weak or childish. She knows she can count on me to help support us all. I am strong, and Ida knows that. So do I—I guess.*

Soon came the call for supper. I jumped up and ran down the back stairs to the kitchen. I was late! Never thought to pack our picnic! But Ida hadn't forgotten. She handed me a basket packed with all we needed, and I took Vivian and her bear up to my room for a quiet evening. She was glad to go with me, especially after she saw the toys I'd assembled. The Alice doll, which she promptly named Mommy, was her favorite. The wild golden hair was indeed reminiscent of her mother's beautiful, unruly mane. I felt a sharp pang, but I managed to keep my grief to myself.

We all sat together on the bed for our picnic. Vivian was especially solicitous of the doll and the bear, offering them bits of bread, chicken, and carrots by turn. All three of them, I noticed, were sloppy eaters. I'd have to be careful to clean off the bed—and the floor around it—before I attempted to lie down for the night.

After supper, it was time for Vivian to go to bed in Lucy's room. Vivian's little bed had already been made up, and her pink nightgown was spread out upon it. I helped her get ready for bed, with Cherry Bearie and Mommy already tucked in. But then Vivian decided that Mommy needed a bed of her own. She insisted that we bring a load of blocks over from my room to make a bed for her. Ceremoniously, she put Mommy to bed, then covered her with a napkin blanket and gave her a kiss. I tucked Vivian and the bear into bed together.

At this point, she admonished the bear: "Hush, Cherry! Mommy needs to sleep!"

"You and Cherry Bearie need to sleep too," I told her as I hugged them both. "You've had a busy day."

PART SIX

END AND BEGINNING

33

Monday, November 4, was our first day back to school. It was also the first time in a month that I got to walk to school with Rosie. I had so much to tell her.

Usually, she comes by at 8:20 on the dot, if not a little before. I donned my mask, gathered up my load of books and papers, and settled on the porch to wait for her. But 8:20 came and went, and there was no sign of Rosie. Was she okay? Oh no! I hoped she hadn't come down with it too!

I checked the parlor clock through the window. Time to go. Iroquois Avenue was empty; most of the students would have arrived at school already. I raced the last block, arrived just before the bell that would send students pouring out of homerooms on their way to their first classes. I ran up to my homeroom, slipped into my seat, shoved some books into the desk, and kept the ones I'd need for the morning's classes.

Whew! I had been in such a rush that I hadn't had time to scan the room or check in with my friends before the bell sent us tearing off to our first classes.

It wasn't until lunchtime that I had a chance to check in with Rosie—briefly, it turned out—in the cafeteria line.

"Hello, Rosie. I missed you this morning." I tried not to sound too disappointed.

Rosie would have been oblivious whether I'd succeeded or not. She was flying high. "You'll *never* guess who walked me to school this morning!"

It certainly was not I, I thought. Then aloud I asked, "Who could it have been?"

"Harold!"

"He came all the way across town to walk you to school?"

"Well, no. I happened to be on an errand over near where he lives, and he happened to come out of his house just as I walked by."

"What was your errand?"

"Can't talk now!" she said, grabbing her tray so roughly that half her soup sloshed out of the bowl. She giggled and shrugged, then whispered, "Lunch with Harold. You understand!"

And then she was gone. I looked around the lunchroom for someone who would let me sit at their table. Everybody seemed completely wrapped up in their own little social circles. I sat by myself and left the cafeteria early to walk around and around the schoolyard and think.

Nobody interrupted me.

After lunch, I got to turn in my pile of Latin homework. Mrs. Brown was surprised that I had finished the entire fourth year of Latin in a month. "Did you do all of this work *yourself*?"

I persuaded her that my interest in Dido and Aeneas, and in war—along with having Reid as a tutor—had made it easy to sink my teeth into the *Aeneid*. She made me translate a few of the more difficult passages, then decided that I was not trying to pass off Reid's work as my own.

"No one in my experience—even young Reid—has accomplished so much Latin learning in so short a time," she told me. "Have you considered college?"

College is for boys, not me, I thought, though I kept that thought to myself. But I tucked her suggestion away at the back of my mind.

At the end of the day Rosie and I did get to walk home together. (Harold, she said, had basketball practice.)

Rosie was gushing with news. "I couldn't tell you at lunch, Ellie, but this morning, I got up early. I told my mother I had time to deliver a quart of her homemade applesauce to Great Aunt Lydia, who just *happens* to live right up the street from Harold's family. I chatted with Aunt Lydia at the door until I saw Harold step out onto the street. Then I told her I had to rush off to school. I just *happened* to reach the sidewalk at the moment Harold was passing by."

"Good timing," I told her as soon as I could get a word in edgewise.

"He *likes* me, Ellie!" And then she went on to tell me—at length—all the signs and indications from which she'd drawn this conclusion. I couldn't look down my nose at her for that; I'd done the same thing, but in the privacy of my own head. I hoped she wouldn't be disappointed.

We arrived at our house before I had a chance to tell her anything about the horrors that my family had been through over the past month. Another time, I would have walked Rosie home and continued our conversation, but today I had to leave her. I needed to relieve Lucy from her day's duties as Vivian's nursemaid.

Lucy was glad to see me. "She's a sweet girl, but active! I've had to chase her around the house all day to keep her out of trouble. I finally let her play with pots and pans in the kitchen. She turned them all into percussion instruments—made enough noise to wake the dead! But at least she didn't break anything. This time."

So I took charge of Vivian while Lucy disappeared into the quiet of her room until dinnertime.

The rest of the week was full of unexpected turns. On Thursday afternoon, just as Mrs. Ivens was beginning our English class, a growing ruckus of shouting, tooting of horns, wailing of sirens, and ringing of church bells drowned out whatever she had started to say. Most of the noise came through the windows from the streets around the school, but some of the hubbub came from the hallway too.

Then the door opened abruptly—it was Mr. Silas, the principal. "The war is over! The Armistice is signed!" he cried. "The Armistice is signed! All classes dismissed! The Armistice is signed!" A stampede of excited students streamed down the hall behind him.

Mrs. Ivens stood agog as we all jumped up and poured out of the room, adding our own voices to the rest of the hollering crowd that was heading toward the exit. One of the first out the door was Harold, who leapt onto a chair and grabbed the American flag that hung near the classroom door just before he took off.

"Don't worry, Mrs. Ivens," he called out behind him. "I'll bring it back!"

Outside, the revelry was even more chaotic. The whole town, it seemed, was in the street and whooping with joy. A couple of automobiles that were stuck among the celebrating horde joined right in with their Klaxon horns, and all the dogs in town barked along. A horse and wagon were caught near the edge of the uproar. The poor horse spooked and ran away with its alarmed driver, scattering the crowd in front of it. Bowler hats, workmen's caps, and even a few ladies' feathered chapeaus flew through the air and ended up trampled on the ground—all except for one, which perched like a bird at the top of a flag waver's pole.

The celebration looked as if it would go on forever. But then Mayor Heinz mounted the hotel steps, tried to hush the crowd, and shouted out, "Go home! Go back to work! There has been a mistake!

The Armistice is coming, but it has not yet arrived! Stay calm, everyone!"

His announcement was slow at first to have an effect, but soon, as people passed the news further and further into the crowd, the shouting quieted and the disappointed revelers began to disperse. At last it became possible for me to pull myself away and walk slowly home along crowded Iroquois Avenue.

I think we all felt a little let down after the hoopla, but I remembered what Francis had said in his letter back in October: *The war is nearly over. I know it!*

Now I did too.

34

The *real* Armistice came only four days after the false one. This time, Foersterville's celebration was a lot less giddy than before. We'd had a bit of time to get used to the idea of peace, I suppose, and our excitement had mellowed into a quieter, deeper joy. There was a big crowd, but it was more sedate—no parade, no whooping in the streets, just a small brass band playing patriotic songs on the hotel steps—and the certainty of another of Mayor Heinz's endless orations. Once again, we got out of school for the occasion, though this time Mr. Silas informed us we'd have to make up for all of this fall's breaks by shortening our Christmas, Easter, and even summer vacations.

I did not tarry on my way home. By the time I got there, Ida had already settled into the big green rocker on the front porch, wrapped in a warm quilt. She was smiling and waving to all the passersby. I've rarely seen her so merry. I stepped inside to drop my books in the front hall before joining her on the porch.

Mom was on the telephone, having an animated discussion with somebody. We waved to each other from opposite ends of the hall, and I slipped back out to sit on the front step next to Ida. Pretty soon, Lucy came out, too, along with Vivian, who was so bundled up she could barely move. Lucy settled into a porch chair and lifted Vivian onto her lap. Vivian sat quietly while the three of us chatted. She didn't squirm as she always does when I hold her but leaned against Lucy, looking very much at home. *Lucy will be a good mother someday*, I thought.

Soon after, along came Reid, racing up the Verona Street hill. "Just the folks I was hoping to see!" he cried as he rounded the corner and spotted us on the porch. "This is the day I've been waiting for!" I'd never seen him so unguarded, so downright gleeful. It was charming, actually.

"Tell us your news, dear," said Ida, gesturing for him to sit down beside her.

"It's the same news that brings you all out in the cold today. The Great War is over! But for me, it means even more than that. Today is the end of the *draft*—and the beginning of my new life. I've been waiting so long for this day. Years!"

"That's fine, Reid," said Lucy. "Do you know when you'll be leaving for college?"

"The dean told me I can start as soon as I'm available. The next term begins at the end of February, so my plan is to start then. In the meantime, I'll have more than plenty to do to get ready—clearing out my little shack, to begin with!"

"You mean, getting rid of all your *books*?" I was horrified.

"Do you want them, kiddo?"

I had to laugh. My room is even smaller than his little shack, and it was already crammed with stuff. It was *Reid* I'd been thinking about, not me. "Those books seem so important to you, Reid. It would be a shame for you to give them all up. Besides, you may need some of them in college."

Lucy had a suggestion. "Can you take them up to your parents' place?"

It was Reid's turn to laugh. "Hell, no! Their place is not much bigger than mine. And it leaks like a sieve. So taking them up there would be the same as throwing them away. Only harder—I'd have to lug them all up the hill first."

I had an idea. "Promise that you won't do anything about the books for the next few days. I can't guarantee anything in return, but there may be a solution."

"Okay, Eleanor. I have plenty of other chores to keep me busy in the meantime."

Interesting, I thought. *That's the first time he's ever called me by my real name.*

Lucy, who was sitting closest to the door, piped in. "I think Mom is off the telephone now," she said. "Ellie, can you manage Vivian for a minute? I need to ask her a question." She disappeared inside and then popped right back out again. "Ida," she said, "do we have enough dinner to feed one or two extra people today?"

"There's *always* enough for a few guests, Lucy. Whom do you have in mind?"

"Reid, to begin with. Reid, will you join us for dinner?"

"A nice warm dinner in a nice warm house—with a nice warm family? I'd be honored, Lucy!"

"Wonderful!" she said. "Will you run down to John's with me, Reid? I want to invite him too."

Reid nodded, then gave me a sly wink. "A *preprandial* perambulation? It'll be my pleasure."

I had to giggle.

As the two of them set off, Ida and I, taking Vivian with us, went back into the house to make the final dinner preparations. I set the table for eight—no, nine of us, with Vivian's high chair tucked between Lucy's and Doc's places. Ida tended the pot roast, Vivian merrily bashed pots and pans together, and Mom sat at her little kitchen writing desk, dashing off what looked to me like some kind of outline. Mom is quite a wonder—she has always been able to keep her focus in the midst of chaos. But she did permit me to interrupt her long enough to ask her one quick question. She gave me a nod and a smile in return. Reid would find out about our exchange when he came back.

Soon the men began arriving. First came Doc, who swept the gleeful, squealing Vivian into his arms and carried her off to the parlor (without her pots and pans) for a quiet cuddle before dinner. Then Pop arrived, settling in the parlor with Doc, and finally Lucy, John, and Reid. Those three headed for the kitchen, where John embraced all of us womenfolk before retiring to the parlor with the other men, and Reid thanked Mom for opening her home to him on this auspicious day. She accepted his thanks with a smile that looked quite genuine to me. She seemed to have softened considerably toward Reid since the last time he had dinner with us.

As we all sat down at the table, Mom took something from the mantle and placed it on the table between her and Ida. It turned out to be the photograph that John and I had taken of Francis just before he shipped off to war.

"He's with us in spirit," she told us. "Soon he'll be with us in the flesh—but until then, his picture will remain on the table to remind us all of our beloved son, brother, nephew, friend."

"Amen," said Pop.

"Amen," we all repeated before digging into Ida's delicious pot roast.

Mom began the dinner conversation. "Tell us about your college plans, Reid. The girls let me know that you will start your studies in February."

Reid was on his best behavior. "Yes, Mrs. Foerster. I have been accepted at Rensselaer Polytechnic Institute, RPI. I'll be studying to become an engineer."

Mom looked surprised. "Trains? That requires college?"

"Not that kind of engineer, ma'am. I want to be an *electrical* engineer. I want to learn about radio, a communications miracle that will change our lives. Imagine listening to, say, an opera at the same time that it is being sung in New York—without getting up from your living room chair. Imagine hearing President Wilson give a speech in Washington at the very moment he utters it. Imagine being able to listen anywhere—even in a cabin up on Yankee Hill!"

I had never seen Reid so passionately wound up in anything. Even Latin! But then, radio did sound pretty exciting.

Mom smiled. "Eleanor tells me you have a large collection of books in your little cabin, and that you have no place to store them when you leave for college."

"That's true, Mrs. Foerster."

"Out in the barn, there is a horse stall that has been disused for several years. Would you like to keep your books there until you have space for them? We never lock the barn, so you could come and go as you please."

"I appreciate your offer, Mrs. Foerster, but I have no way to pay rent for the space."

"No, no, Reid. There would be no rental fee. The space is yours as long as you need it. Isn't that correct, Arthur?"

Pop startled a bit, I thought. This whole idea was new to him. I knew that for a fact since I'd suggested the idea to Mom just before Pop arrived for dinner. "Why, of course, Lily. Just as you say. It's the least we can do to support this ambitious young fellow!"

Once the future of Reid's books was assured, Mom went on to tell us about the garden club's latest project, erecting a "Victory

Arch"—either over Iroquois Avenue or over Verona Street, which is narrower and thus somewhat easier to span.

"I say we go for Iroquois," said Pop. "It *is* the main business street in town, the pride of Foersterville! It would take a broad span, yes, but no broader than my mill or a dozen dairy barns all over the county. We can find a way to build that arch."

Mom brightened. "I'm happy to hear that, dear. Can you take charge of designing it?"

"I may need some help," said Pop. "Maybe Muller or Welk or the fellows down at the sawmill."

"While you're at it, you might ask the sawmill if they can donate the lumber to make it."

"Good idea," said Pop. Then he fell quiet. I think it dawned on him that he had just agreed to take charge of the whole construction project.

Reid was the next volunteer. "I can help with the sawing and hammering. Lord knows I've done enough of it in my day. And maybe I could find a way to add some electric lights to the arch."

"That's very good of you," Mom replied. "Especially since you have so much to do as you prepare for college. I remember going through a similar process myself back when I began my studies at the conservatory."

Doc joined in. "I'm close by. I can help, too, whenever I'm not seeing patients."

"How do you plan to decorate that wooden arch once it's built, Mom?" Lucy asked.

"Bunting, to start with. Yards and yards of bunting. Beyond that, flowers. Red, white, and blue flowers. After all, we are the garden club."

"But it's November, Mom! There *are* no flowers at this time of year."

"To be sure," she responded. "We are trying to work that out now. Perhaps we can use paper flowers until the growing season begins."

"Paper wouldn't survive winter rain and snow," Ida pointed out. "There may be another material that would be more durable."

Lucy had a flash of inspiration. "Oilcloth! Could we fashion oilcloth into believable flowers?"

"It would be worth a try," said Ida. "Let us experiment to see if we can make a pattern for all the volunteers to use."

"This Victory Arch will be quite the project!" said John. "With your permission, Lily, I'd like to take photographs of all the volunteers as you create it. It will make an interesting historical record."

"You certainly may, John."

"I'll need your help, Ellie. Will you be my assistant?"

"I'll help with *everything*! The building, the decorating, the photographing—it all sounds like great fun!"

The victory dinner proved to be a big victory in itself for Mom. She'd rounded us all up as volunteers for her grand new project.

35

Helping with *everything* on the Victory Arch project was a bit more than I could manage, as it happened. When I had made that promise, I'd forgotten all about school, which had been closed for Armistice Day. I'd have to limit my contributions to weekends.

But Ida got busy right away. She persuaded Braun Brothers' store to donate yards and yards of white oilcloth, which she and Lucy fashioned into carnations and lilies for the arch. They were careful to draw patterns and work out step-by-step instructions for the garden club volunteers to use in making their own flowers. By the time the weekend came, all that was left for me to do on that job was to test their instructions by making my own flowers from the patterns. My lily turned out fine, but the best you could say of the carnation was that it would be a blur from fifteen feet below. After Lucy edited the instructions a bit, my second carnation turned out pretty well.

Pop cleared out a space on the ground floor of the barn to accommodate building the arch and its supports. He drew a design and checked it with friends who had more experience than he in barn raising. By the weekend, he had all the wood, tools, and volunteers he needed to execute his plan.

John had already taken photographs of Ida and Lucy as they designed the flowers. Later, I could help him photograph the carpenters building the arch and the garden club ladies decorating it. I also thought there should be a whole group picture of everyone who volunteered time or materials. John said that was a good idea. He told me the *Journal* would like it too: "The more local citizens we put in our pictures, the more papers they sell," he explained. "And the more business I get. That's what capitalism is all about, Ellie: selling more and more."

Things were happening at school as well as at home. At the beginning of Latin class on Monday, Mrs. Brown returned all of our October homework, graded. I wasn't surprised at the good grade I got. What did surprise me was a note that she handed to me at the same time:

> *Please go to the principal's office.*
> *You are excused from my class today.*
> *Helen Brown*

I looked up at her, trying to fathom in her face the meaning of this odd message. Her bland look revealed nothing.

"Now?" I asked. She nodded calmly. No information in that look.

"Okay. Um . . . *Vale, magistra!*" She has always insisted on formal Latin farewells at the end of class.

"*Vale, discipula.*"

Mr. Silas was waiting at his office door when I arrived. As he ushered me in, I noticed that both my *parents* were already there. I thought, *What have I done?*

"Please have a seat." He gestured to a chair next to where Pop had settled.

"I need to report to you what I have just discussed with your father and mother," he said gravely. "Mrs. Brown showed me the work you did for Latin IV during the recent hiatus. She feels that you have shown enough mastery of the entire course that you should be credited with having completed it as of today. I have been discussing the matter with your parents, and we all agree that this would be the best plan for you."

Oh. This should have been good news, getting permission to play hooky with the principal's blessing—and Mom and Pop's as well. But I felt kind of annoyed.

I'm sure I would have made the same decision myself, but it really bothered me that they'd made it all on their own, without even consulting me. Still, I tried to put the best face on the situation. After all, not having to go to Latin class did give me an extra study period at the end of every day. The only question was *what* I'd study.

Mom and Pop were silent through Mr. Silas's announcement. I suspected he had cowed them when *they* were students at Foersterville High too. As soon as we were dismissed, though, Mom looked as if she were about to burst.

"Oh, my baby!" she said. "I'm so proud of you!"

"Thank you, Mom," I responded politely.

Pop joined in. "You've brought honor to your family, Eleanor."

This is a mystery to me. What was the pride and honor in finishing a course a few months early? Why was it such a wonder that I liked reading old Roman stories?

Being excused from Latin class for the whole rest of the year gave me an hour-long study hall at the end of each school day. That seemed absurd to me. Why would I need *more* time to study for *fewer* classes? Maybe it was because nobody had thought about what *else* I might do during that time. Come to think of it, neither had I.

I found an answer just an hour later.

On my way home from school, I did my first marketing errand for John, stopping by Mr. Lloyd's shop to show him proofs of our first photos from the Victory Arch project: volunteers drawing up plans, laying out lumber for the structure, and designing, sewing, and assembling the garlands of cloth flowers and foliage that would decorate it. John wanted to know whether Mr. Lloyd was willing to sell the images as postcards to benefit the garden club.

"What a fine historical record of Foersterville's patriotic spirit! This project deserves a whole series of postcards that follow it from start to finish—and a *book* of the photographs as well, with explanatory text. It will be a treasure for all the families of Iroquois County, not just the garden club."

"Mr. Lloyd? Am I correct in thinking that timing is important on this project?"

"Most certainly so! The sooner you can complete it, the better!"

"Well, I have an extra study hall at the end of the school day. Mr. Silas might be persuaded to let me out early to work with John on an important project like this one. Could you bring it up with him?"

"As it happens, I'll be seeing Silas at Rotary Club tomorrow. I shall propose it to him as a special project!"

I skipped all the way home.

Evidently, Mr. Lloyd was persuasive. The very next afternoon, I got permission to skip my afternoon study hall until this project was done—or until the end of the semester—whichever came first.

While Mom and Pop stayed busy overseeing the building of the arch, I helped John photograph the whole process of erecting and decorating it—and then develop the pictures quickly, making sure we had good shots of all the steps along the way. There were some scary moments as the men raised the heavy, awkward structure over Iroquois Avenue, but luckily, we never had to photograph an accident scene.

By the time the arch was up and finished, just before the

holidays, Mom was already planning to create replacements for the decorations as they weathered over the winter. She believed it would be some while before we welcomed the last soldiers home. The new recruits, those who had just begun their training at nearby camps, were already beginning to trickle in, but we didn't expect to see the troops come back from the front for a month or two yet.

On Saturday came the letter from Francis that we'd all been waiting for. I'd been hoping he'd tell us that he was coming home right away, maybe in time for Christmas. Pop read the letter to all of us at dinner:

Dear Mom and Pop and all,

I'm back with my unit again, at least for a while. We're in easternmost France, almost on the border with Germany. The boys sure did make some progress while I healed up at the hospital. I got back to my unit just before they signed the Armistice, and just in time for the biggest celebration folks around here have ever had.

Most of the boys are getting ready to head home, but the sergeant picked me and a few other boys to go to Germany with the occupying forces. They want us to serve as military police. It could be six months until we're discharged. That will make me the first Foersterville boy to join up—and no doubt the last Foersterville man to come home!

At least we few "laggers" won't be dodging flying bullets and shells all the time.

I miss you!

Your loving

Francis

"At least he's safe," Ida commented. We all had to agree. But Mom sighed at the thought that her eldest child and only son would be stuck in Europe for six long months.

That afternoon, while I sat at my desk to catch up on my homework, I heard the barn door creak open below. I looked out the window to see Reid pulling a wheelbarrow-load of his books inside. He was starting to fill up his little storeroom. I'd been wanting to talk to him—this would be a good time to go over and see if I could help. He accepted my offer happily.

Reid had lined the whole stall with bookshelves. "I made them out of leftover scraps from the arch," he told me. "Now they're ready to be loaded up. But first, we have to sort the books." He laid out a row of paper labels on the worktable across from his stall. Each one was neatly printed with the name of a topic: *Agriculture*, *Botany*, *Business*, *Classics*, *Electricity*, *History*, and on through the alphabet to *Zoology*. My job, he told me, was to place the books in piles by subject while he fetched the next batch from his raft down on the river.

It took him five more trips down to the raft and back before he got the rest of the books into the stall. It was while we were sorting the last batch together that I told him my news.

"I'm done with Latin!" I announced. "Mrs. Brown decided that I have finished the course and don't have to go to class any longer. She got Mr. Silas to go along with her, and he persuaded Mom and Pop. I was mad at first that nobody had asked *me* about it, but now I'm glad to be done."

"No surprise to me, kiddo. You dug right into it. Bowled me over with your enthusiasm!"

"Thank you for helping me through it all."

"Thanks, but you earned your own success, Ellie. Have you ever considered going to college?"

"College? Me? No, it's Francis who'll be going to college, once he gets back from the war."

"I think *you* should."

It was getting to be too dark to sort books, even in the light of a streetlamp outside the open door. We decided to call it a day. It was time for me to set the supper table anyway.

We said our farewells at the corner and went our separate ways—Reid to his chilly cabin on the river and me to the warmth of Ida's kitchen.

When I arrived, I was surprised to see she wasn't alone. John was there, too, leaning comfortably back in his chair at the table, visiting with her while she stood at the stove. She was stirring the white sauce for tonight's supper of dried-beef gravy on toast.

"What brings you here, John?" I asked.

"I stopped by to chat after a session at the Masonic Temple," he said, gesturing toward the load of photographic equipment by the back door. "Ida was kind enough to ask me to stay for supper.

"Have I ever turned down one of her meals? Not within living memory, I haven't!"

"I'm glad for that," I said. "I need your advice, both of you. Reid thinks I should go to college!"

"Good idea!" said John, sitting straight up in his chair.

"What do you think, Ida?"

She went on calmly stirring her gravy pot. "There's no question you have the talent for it, dear. But is it something *you* want to do?"

"I don't know. I never thought seriously about it until just now. I look at Reid, who seems to know exactly what he wants to learn and how he wants to use it afterward. *I* don't have anything like his certainty about my own future."

"Few young people do. But he may surprise himself and go off in an entirely different direction once he discovers all the other things he can learn in college. In my teaching days, I had students who wanted to master one particular subject, and I had students who wanted to learn *everything.* I suspect that you fall into the latter category."

After supper was over and Vivian was put to bed, I asked Lucy to sit with me for a bit in the quiet of my room. I need to talk with her about this college business.

She stretched out on my bed. Poor girl—she works hard enough; she needs a little time to relax. I leaned back in the desk chair with my feet propped up on the foot of the bed. She smiled when I told her I was thinking of going to college.

"I would never have considered college for myself. For you, though, it might well be worth thinking about," she said. "Me, I'm a homebody, like Pop, but you're more adventurous, like Mom. You're full of ambition, just like her."

"Mom? I've never thought of her as adventurous, exactly."

"How many local people do you know who've ever gone all the way to New York City to become an *opera singer,* of all things? What a courageous move that was!"

"But then she came home after a year or two and married Pop. She never did finish her training."

"Have you ever asked her why?"

Maybe I should.

36

Mom was always so busy with her community projects, or her clubs, or her music, that it was hard to find time for a quiet conversation with her. But I kept looking for an opening, and one day, it came along as we were making the beds together upstairs.

"Were you planning to go to the conservatory when you moved down from the hill, Mom?"

"No, dear. I was just fourteen when I came here. I didn't even know what a conservatory was! My plan was to finish school and go back to Yankee Hill as a teacher. But then I started singing in the church choir. And *then* I started taking voice lessons from a kind music teacher who thought I had promise. It was she who introduced me to opera and encouraged me to go to conservatory when I finished high school. It took a great deal of hard work, but I did succeed—in *starting* my conservatory training, at least."

"Did you like it there?"

"At first I was homesick, but that didn't last long. There was so much to learn—about the wonderful music all around me, my talented new classmates, the brilliant professors, the city itself! I came to love everything about it."

"But Mom, why did you leave if you loved it so much?"

"I loved your father too. And he asked me to marry him."

"Wouldn't he have waited for you to finish your schooling?"

"I didn't know for certain at the time, but I believed there was a good chance Arthur would choose someone else if I asked him to wait two more years for my graduation. You see, his parents had recently died, and he had just inherited both the family house and the mill. He told me he needed a wife to help him manage all this new responsibility."

By now we had finished our chores, but not Mom's account. She gestured for us to settle in the little sitting area at the head of the stairs. Then she sighed and went on: "I had watched some of my predecessors at the conservatory—very talented musicians—struggle and fail to make a name for themselves as professionals, waiting too long to marry, ending up both poor and lonely. I went over and over the choices in my mind: either settle down now and give up any hope of a future in opera, or finish my education and lose my chance at family, love, and security while trying for a career that was almost certain to fail anyway. In the end, the choice was easy."

"Are you glad you made the choice you did, Mom?"

"Of *course*!" she said a little shrilly. "Isn't it *obvious*?"

It was obvious to me that the conversation was over. She was not about to reveal anything more.

I wonder if I would have made the same decision that Mom did.

37

For little Vivian's sake, the rest of us did our best to make Christmas jolly, but it was hard.

Doc would give Vivian a goodnight kiss after supper each night. Then Lucy would take her upstairs, tuck her into bed, and retreat to the old rocking chair at the top of the stairs. She would sit there silently in the dark for an hour or more, until she was certain that Vivian was fast asleep. Then Lucy would go off to bed herself. It was clear to everyone that she did not want to be disturbed in the evenings. These days, Vivian was her only reason to keep going.

Doc, on the other hand, seemed to need our company. He joined the rest of us in the parlor, sitting on the settee next to Ida. His conversation drifted toward happy memories of Cora.

He talked about how they had met, while they were both in training at a hospital in Albany: "I ran into Cora—*literally*—one afternoon at the hospital. I was trotting along the corridor, afraid I would be late for a meeting. I got to a corner, and *bam*! There she was, on her way to tend to a patient. We knocked each other to the floor before we ever saw each other. After helping each other up and seeing that neither of us was hurt, we went on our separate ways—but not before she had agreed to let me walk her home at the end of our shift. We've been together ever since."

Doc started to sigh, but his sigh turned into a choking sob. Ida reached over and embraced him until the sobbing faded.

"Thank you, Ida," he said as his voice began to come back. "Thank you all. You help make this pain bearable."

Sharing the grief made it more bearable for all of us, I think, at least until we went off to our own beds.

Then the ghosts of Will and Cora took over.

I couldn't quite feel the book of Millay poems that Will had given me last year, but I knew it was right under my mattress. It was all I could do to keep from reaching in to pull it out and stoke my agony all over again.

I looked out the window toward the river and the tracks beyond.

All these losses. How long would they go on?

38

The only bright spot of this dreary season was that John's and my photographs of the arch project—especially the little book—were bestsellers at Mr. Lloyd's store. His theory was that the books were perfectly timed to serve as Christmas gifts. Everybody in town, it seemed, got one in her stocking. Including me!

Right at the end of the holiday, Mom came to me with a proposal. She said, "I am exceedingly proud of the good use you have made of your time since you got permission to leave school early each day. Would you like to continue doing so?"

"Boy, *would I!*" Looking back, I wish I'd asked what she had in mind before responding so enthusiastically.

"Your father and I have been talking. One of the girls in his office—Abigail, the bookkeeper—is leaving soon. She met a nice, prosperous young farmer, one of your father's suppliers, to whom she will soon be married. What a fine opportunity for you to learn a bit about your father's business—and perhaps meet your own young man as well!"

"No."

"That was abrupt, dear! You would work only in the afternoons, just as you did for my brother John. And unlike with John, you would be earning money as you learn."

"I'm sorry I offended you, Mom. You surprised me."

"Well, think about it, dear. You'll never have Lucy's marriage opportunities—not unless you develop your social skills and meet some likely prospects."

Just to mollify her I told her that I would mull it over.

I wish that Mom could understand me. I wish I could persuade her that I have other goals besides marriage, at least for now. Seeing the world beyond Foersterville. Seeing the world through books and ideas. Seeing the world through the lens of a camera.

Soon after my talk with Mom, a blizzard left over three feet of snow in Foersterville. It made all the streets and roads impassable for miles around, shutting down all of Iroquois County. Even making progress on sidewalks was treacherous. The storm had started with heavy snow, which was followed by a layer of sleet that formed a hard, slippery crust on top. The sleet also formed icicles that sparkled from trees and roofs and telephone lines once morning arrived and the sun came out. As soon as John awoke the day after the storm, he decided this magical scene was a great opportunity for postcard photographs. He invited me to go with him as his assistant.

We trudged together through snow and ice all over town, which was still quiet and deserted at that hour, taking photographs of all the lovely snowy, icy sights while they were still pristine: unmelted, untouched by traffic, undirtied by the coal ash from everyone's furnaces. It was hard, cold work, but oh my, it was beautiful.

The next day, John and I worked together to develop and print our photographs. As always, we chatted in the darkroom.

"Did you hear about the big strike out in Seattle?" he asked as we worked.

"No, John. Tell me about it."

"It started with shipyard workers, who wanted to get paid a fair wage. They asked other unions to join them. Soon, it turned into a general strike that has scared the daylights out of the powers that be. More power to those workers, I say!"

"Did they get what they wanted?"

"Not yet. At this point, too many people are hollering at them: 'Bolshevik! Red! Communist!' The hollerers haven't figured out yet that these fellows just want a job that gives them food and clothing and a future for their families. They just call them names and ignore the facts. That suits the bosses just fine."

Unfortunately for John, he made this same argument in a letter he wrote to the *Foersterville Journal*. The aftermath was almost instant. The day after the paper came out, the school board held a special meeting to decide whether to stop using him as its photographer.

Two days later, John showed up at the back door as Ida and I were cleaning up after breakfast. He held out a letter in a sealed envelope.

"This just got slipped under my door," he told us. "It arrived as I was about to set off on some errands. Thought I'd stop by and read it here. With you."

Was that a little tremor in his voice? He slit the envelope open with a table knife that had been lying on the drainboard, withdrew the single page, and read us the letter. It was from the school board.

> *. . . For some time, the Board has had concerns about repeated rumors of your Bolshevist leanings, among them that you had advocated for the unionization of local businesses, had expressed unpatriotic pacifist views, and had abetted draft evasion during the late war. The Board let these matters pass, believing them to be but rumors and not wishing to move precipitously in response.*
>
> *Your recent letter, published in the current issue of the Foersterville Journal, has erased any doubts the Board may*

have entertained as to your opinions. It has been agreed that the children of this village must be protected from your influence; therefore, it has been determined that the Foersterville Central School District shall no longer require your services as school photographer.

Ida shook her head sadly. "Alas, dear boy, though I agree with your views, it seems you have more passion than good sense. I fear you will suffer further for it." Then she reached out to give him a reassuring pat. "But you are smart and resourceful too. You will find a way to succeed in your work without sacrificing your beliefs."

"I hope to *hell* that's true!"

The school board's action was only the beginning of the unraveling of John's business. A couple of days later, when he went to the stationery store to sell the lovely winter postcards we had just taken, Mr. Lloyd refused to even look at them. Nobody would buy anything with John's name on it, he announced.

It took only a few weeks for John's income to dry up completely. Families stopped hiring him to record their engagements, weddings, baptisms, and funerals. Even the *Journal* declined to publish his pictures. He began to realize there was nothing left of the career he had spent so long to build. As popular and successful as he had been in Foersterville, nobody wanted to associate with him anymore. He was too dangerous.

If John hadn't been facing such disastrous consequences for telling people his political beliefs, I'd have laughed to think that anyone regarded him as dangerous. After all, I hear his opinions almost every day, and I'm none the worse for it. He makes me think.

Was it wrong for John to "abet" Reid in avoiding the draft? After all, it led to Reid's setting up the most productive truck farm in the county, one that still feeds Foersterville well—and it will for a long time to come if Mr. Muller is willing to keep it going. It's also true that Reid took advantage of the situation in order to hang on to his hopes for an education, but he did it by performing a real service to the country. Was that *undermining* the war effort or *supporting* it?

Was it wrong for John to think the seamstresses at Ben Dowd's shirtwaist factory get worked too hard and paid too little, so they should band together to demand the money and respect they deserve? After all, even Mom had had to remind Mr. Dowd that his employees were grown *women*, not *girls*.

If these are Bolshevist ideas, then maybe Mom's a Bolshevist too. And maybe *I* am. I suppose we'd all best keep our mouths shut around Foersterville.

Dinner on Sunday turned into a planning meeting. What was next for John?

"I can't stay here in town," he told us.

"Where might you go?" Mom asked. I was expecting him to propose Oneonta, a bigger town down the road from us, or Albany, the nearest city. He surprised us all.

"Out West."

"You mean Syracuse?" Mom asked. Syracuse is the farthest west that any of us has ever been. Unless Oswego is.

"No, Washington State. Oregon. California. *Way* out West."

"In Heaven's name, *why*?"

John settled back in his chair. "Things are happening out on the West Coast. Unions are strong. Progressive thinkers are plentiful—and they're not generally forced into silence, like around here. I need to go to a place where I can say what I believe without being muzzled for it."

As Mom tried mightily to persuade him to change his mind (to no avail), I sat there stunned at the bravery—or was it recklessness?—of his decision to abandon everything in his past and make a whole new life for himself.

"But there's nothing left of my old life," he pointed out. "I destroyed it myself by blurting out my true beliefs. No businessman can get away with that in a small town like Foersterville."

Pop nodded sagely. "I've always said that you risk losing half your business by running for office. Too many people on the other side will take offense."

Mom jumped in. "But John, you went even beyond that and alienated them *all*. If you were not my little brother, I wouldn't want to do business with you myself."

"Water over the dam," said Ida quietly. "They say the West is beautiful."

After that, the talk turned to practical matters.

John had saved up enough money to pay train fare and stay in a boardinghouse for a few months while he got settled. Pop would manage selling his house and auctioning off the goods he left behind. I'd help him pack his equipment before he left.

I knew I'd miss him greatly.

39

I was tempted to dawdle along in my new chore of helping John get ready to leave. He's my uncle, my friend, and my teacher; it pained me to watch him go so far away that I might never see him again. But he needed to leave, and soon. I couldn't spoil his future.

I'd started working at John's house every day after school, and on weekends, too, helping him go through all his stuff to figure out what he needed to take with him, what he'd need after he got settled, and what he'd never want again.

Our first task was to make a portfolio so that he could show his best photographs to people who might hire him. That meant sorting through every print and negative, throwing some away, reprinting some, and separating some out for family and friends. The very best ones he saved in a handsome leather case that he would carry with him when he left.

Seeing those pictures from the past all at once was hard. John had started taking photographs of the family when he was in high school and I was just a baby. My favorite was taken not by him, but by someone else—Mom? Pop?—with John's first camera. It shows him as a young man and me as a little girl, standing together down by the river. His hand rests on my shoulder and I snuggle against him, hugging his leg with all my might. Even back then, John was an idol to me. How I wished I could go with him on his big adventure.

The equipment in John's studio and darkroom came next. Once we'd discarded the empty bottles of chemicals and other trash, the job turned out to be much easier than I'd expected.

"I can't lug my whole darkroom with me out West," John announced as we looked over all the stuff he'd acquired during the past ten years or so. "Maybe I'll send for it when I get my own studio, but meanwhile I'll just have to buy time in someone else's." So the darkroom would go to storage in our barn, at least for the time being. John offered to help me set it up in the stall next to Reid's so that I could use it in the meantime.

He'd already figured out which equipment he needed to take: his favorite camera—the one he uses for all his portrait work—along with its tripod and lenses and plates. Those things he placed carefully in his big black trunk, cushioned by the clothing and linens he wouldn't need until he got to . . . *wherever* he was going. He would also take a smaller camera in the valise that he would carry with him on the train.

"I'll be passing through some spectacular scenery," he told me. "The Great Lakes. The Plains. The desert. The Rocky Mountains. I want to capture all of it on film as I go. I'll be catching those photographs on the fly, so they probably won't turn out to be my best shots. But I hope they'll give you a sense of what it's like to go across the whole country—'from sea to shining sea,' as the song says."

"Send us the whole lot of them, John! Even the ones that don't turn out. Seeing your pictures is the closest I'll ever come to making that trip!"

"Maybe it is, but you never know. It hadn't crossed my mind to go west myself—until I got kicked out of here."

John got Reid to help us with the last part of his preparations, dealing with the furniture. We moved the stuff into two rooms.

Everything that John wanted to save—and possibly ship out West—went into his parlor downstairs, at least for now. Reid would transport it in his trusty wheelbarrow to our barn, where it would be safe until John needed it sent to him. Everything else, the things John wanted to sell or give away, went to his dining room. Pop would arrange its disposal from there.

Finally, the sorting job was all done. Everything John might want in the future was tucked into our barn. Everything he would take with him was packed into his trunk and valise. Everything he wanted to sell or give away was in his dining room. He would be leaving on the train tomorrow morning. It was time for our last dinner together before his journey.

Mom did not mind that Reid joined us for dinner. She was getting used to him, almost as if he were a family member himself.

Ida cooked up a feast for John on the eve of his leaving: chicken and biscuits, sweet potatoes, string beans, gingerbread with whipped cream. It was a delightful evening, but it was also tinged with the sadness of anticipating his departure. I wished it would never end.

Just as we were beginning dessert, John rose to offer a farewell speech. He thanked Mom and Pop for offering him a home in Foersterville, encouraging him to finish his education, and helping him get started as a photographer. He thanked Ida for her wise counsel along the way, and Lucy and me for being friends and sisters as well as nieces. He thanked Reid for showing him the power of raw talent and ambition. He thanked Doc for keeping him well all these years, and Francis (in absentia) for being a little brother to him, a little brother who grew up to be a protector of his nation.

And then he turned to me. "This is for the photographer's apprentice. You've earned your own camera, Ellie."

He handed me a box that he'd pulled out from its hiding place under the table. Inside was a camera, small and compact like the one he took with him for postcard shots around Iroquois County. Looking at it closely, I realized the camera was the *very* one he'd always carried with him on these jaunts.

"John! This is yours! Are you *giving* it to me?" This had been one of his favorite cameras for a long time. If I hadn't already known that, I would have been able to tell by the mellow patina on the brown leather case. It's a beautiful object, and it takes beautiful photographs—at least in John's hands.

"I want you to have it, Ellie. It was given to me by Mr. Bascomb, my boss and photography teacher, when I first came down from Yankee Hill. I bought his studio when he got too old to run it himself. It seems only right that I should pass this camera on to you now that I'm leaving the studio behind. You've been *my* star pupil! Now you can make your own postcards to sell at Mr. Lloyd's. He's already told me he'd happily buy the ones we took right after the blizzard—as long as they have *your* name on them instead of mine. He knows to expect you."

John had given me a beautiful little camera and the chance to earn my own money all at once. I was stunned.

I got to use my camera for the first time the next morning. I got shots of the whole group as we followed Reid, who hauled the wheelbarrow loaded with John's baggage, down the hill to the station. John and Mom, arm in arm, walked right behind him, then Ida and Pop, then Lucy and Doc with little Vivian dancing along between them.

Our little group's mood was surprisingly festive for a family that was ushering their brother, cousin, and friend into exile. I think John had persuaded us all that he was off on an exciting new adventure. I found myself wishing I could go with him.

I did get a few nice photographs at the station, but the station master took the best one of the day. I lent him my camera to take a family portrait of all of us—even Doc, Vivian, and Reid. We're all family now.

Just one week later, it was time for Reid to head off to college. It's true that RPI is only thirty or forty miles away, a lot closer than the West Coast—or Germany, where Francis was still stuck doing military policing. (As far as we knew, anyway, though we hadn't heard from him in months.)

Still, Reid was going away. He might never come back to Foersterville except to pick up his things from the barn—like everyone else, it seemed. I knew I'd miss him, and I thought the whole family would too—even Mom. We're all getting to be experts at missing people. Francis. Will. Cora. John. Even Rosie, who is too focused on Harold to see anything else. And now Reid.

The day of his departure, Reid came by our house to say goodbye. We all chatted in the parlor for a while. Then, when it was time for him to leave for the station, he rose, paused in what looked like embarrassment, and embraced each of us women in turn before shaking hands with Pop and Doc. Vivian got a little kiss.

"Thank you all," he said, his voice breaking a little. "Thank you."

And then he was gone.

It wasn't until both John and Reid had left Foersterville that it occurred to me: Those two are my closest friends. They believe in me, both of them.

The next morning, as I was about to start off for school, the doorbell rang. Rosie! I hadn't had a chance to talk with her in months, not since her obsession with Harold began. I'd missed her company hugely. I wondered if she was finally ready to make room for our friendship again.

Rosie didn't even wait to say hello. We were barely out the door when she started gushing. "You'll never guess what! We talked to Mama, and she said yes, and so we're going to get married! Soon!"

"But Rosie, there's no need to rush. It's more than a year before you graduate," I told her. "You *can't* get married yet."

Sometimes Rosie makes me feel like a bossy older sister.

"Louie won't wait for me to graduate."

"Louie?"

"Louis—or Louise. That's what Harold and I call him—or her. Don't tell a single soul about this, but I'm in the *family* way, Ellie!"

"I suppose they'll soon know, though, whether I tell them or not."

"That's why I want to get married right away, before it shows—much. I want to be able to wear my mama's pretty wedding gown. And I want you to stand up for me! Will you?"

My word! I'd need a little time to think about this.

"Have you set a date?"

"March first, my birthday! Isn't that *sweet*? Father O'Connor will officiate. It'll be a tiny wedding, with just the families—and *you*."

"Thank you for inviting me, Rosie. I need to talk with my family about it first. I'll let you know as soon as I can."

"Okay, but don't tell them about Louie!"

I *couldn't* promise not to mention Louie, but I knew I could trust Mom, Ida, and Lucy to keep Rosie's secret.

Most of all, though, I needed to consult with myself.

I didn't see Harold at school all day. His absence may have been the reason that Rosie was so eager to walk me home that afternoon.

"Harold decided to quit school as soon as Mama told us we'd best marry soon. That was just two days since, though it seems like a million years ago! And he has already found work on the Welk farm, and a place for us to live. He's moving our things into the tenant house over there today. But don't tell anybody about the house, Ellie! I'm in no condition for a shivaree!"

I promised. I was not about to expose her to a band of drunken men banging on pots and pans in the middle of her wedding night, even threatening to carry her away for an hour or two. Shivarees are not as common as they used to be, but they're terrifying even to think about. Yet some men think they're good fun.

Nobody was at home when I arrived. I was just as glad—I needed some time to think about what to do about Rosie. I went upstairs to my room, closed the door behind me, plopped down on the bed, and stared at the ceiling as I tried to think it through. What was the right thing, the *honest* thing, for me to do?

Let's say I believed that Rosie had acted rashly well before she thought. Let's say I was quite sure she wasn't prepared for *any* marriage, especially this one. Let's say I believed that she'd raced into this situation without considering what it meant for her future. Let's say I was pretty sure Harold was even more unprepared for marriage and family than she was. Let's say I cringed when I thought about what a big mistake they were making.

There was no "let's say" about *that* opinion. It's what I really thought!

But there was the hope that I was wrong. Maybe this *was* a good match. Maybe it was more than a crush. Maybe little Louie would have a mother and father who really love each other—and Louie too.

Maybe I should be her attendant after all, I thought, *and maybe that will help make my wish come true.*

But if I didn't *believe* the wish would come true, would it be dishonest for me to act as if it could?

This circle of thought and worry seemed as if it would go on forever. But then I heard boots stomping up the steps to the back door; it brought me back to the present. I trotted downstairs to the kitchen. Mom and Ida had been out shopping together, and Lucy was just back from a walk with little Vivian. I was glad they were all together. Maybe they could help me make up my mind.

"Of course you can't stand up for her under *those* circumstances! *What* would people *think*!"

"They'd think Eleanor was a faithful friend, Mom, who wished the best for Rosie and her new family."

"On the contrary, they would believe she accepts Rosie's shocking behavior! And may have engaged in such wickedness herself!"

"Mom, *you* know—and so does everybody else in Foersterville—she's not that kind of girl. Besides, she's never even had a boyfriend!"

It stung a bit for Lucy to say that about me, even though it was true. But it was even harder to watch Mom and Lucy arguing about me—in the third person—without ever asking *me* what *I* think. I was tempted to go back upstairs and hide in my room for a few days. They might not have even noticed I was gone.

But before I had a chance to do that, Ida spoke up. "What do *you* want to do, dear?"

Thank you, Ida, I thought. *You helped me find my backbone.* I surprised myself when she asked. I knew exactly what I wanted to do—what I *would* do, whether anybody else liked it or not.

"I'm going to stand up for Rosie."

"But Eleanor! What will people think?"

"I don't care what people think, Mom. If they think I'm a—a hussy—for supporting my best friend, they're wrong. I know that, and so do you." I paused. "I wish with all my heart that she and Harold hadn't got themselves into this pickle. But maybe, with help from those around them, they'll be okay. I believe it's the only chance they have."

Mom sighed. "You feel strongly about standing up for your friend—in both senses of the expression. I do not approve of her transgression. I do not approve of your decision. But I will not forbid you from carrying it out."

"Thank you, Mom. Rosie needs all the help she can get."

"And you are brave to offer it, Eleanor."

The wedding, in a small chapel off the main sanctuary, was tiny and quick. Rosie's mother wept through the entire ceremony, and her uncle gave her away. Mel, one of the boys who played on the basketball team with Harold, was the best man. Harold's parents both sat stolidly through the whole thing. Except for Father O'Connor, I was the only other person in attendance. So much for the large disapproving crowd that Mom had anticipated.

I gave Rosie and Harold a hug at the end of the proceedings, and they were gone. Then I went home. They're married.

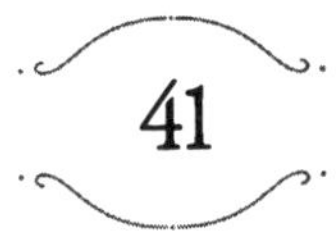

41

John sent us a series of picture postcards (not his own, of course, but those of other photographers) as he made his way out West on the train. The messages were short:

Buffalo stinks, but Lake Erie is vast and beautiful . . .

Chicago is the busiest city I've ever seen . . .

Endless fields! They say this is corn country . . .

Majestic mountains ahead. Hadn't realized how high we've climbed already . . .

Miles and miles of rocks and sand without vegetation. Naked geography!

Soft hills already turning green . . .

Beautiful bay to our west . . .

Oakland is right across the bay from San Francisco. Think I'll stay here. (It's cheaper, they say.)

Found a photographer who is willing to rent me space in her studio. Will send photos soon.

Mom tied all his postcards together with a silver ribbon and tucked them away with Francis's letters in a special drawer of her parlor desk.

Finally! A package from John came in the mail: a scrapbook full of photographs that he'd taken on his trip. They were mounted on black pages with captions John had written in white ink in his artful photographer's hand. We all pored over them—especially me!

The next day, another, smaller package came, this one just for me—though of course I would have let anyone see it who asked. It was full of the photographs that John had chosen not to use in his scrapbook. They weren't captioned, but by comparing the images to the ones he had labeled, I got a pretty good idea of their sequence. I set them out on my bed in order—at least, as close as I could get. They weren't pretty, exactly, but they gave me an idea of what the train trip to California had been like. Most of the photographs showed scenery whizzing past, but there were a few that showed a bit of life on the train—like views of John's upper berth and passengers in the dining car.

I dreamed about the train and its wonders all night long. Someday, maybe I'd go out West on the train myself. *No, not someday*, I suddenly thought. *Soon! As soon as I finish school, as soon as I earn enough money to make the trip—and visit John.*

On my way home from school the next afternoon, I stopped by the train station to find out how much it would cost to travel to California. It turned out it was several times what I'd earned selling postcard photographs to Mr. Lloyd. It would take at least two years at my current pace to bring in enough money to pay for the trip that way. I'd need another source of income.

It got me thinking about how quick I'd been to turn down Mom's idea that I work for Pop, at least until graduation. Her *purpose*—marrying me off—was still anathema to me. But I realized that earning money to do what *I* want suited me perfectly. It wasn't her idea that I hated so much, but her purpose.

I apologized to Mom and told her I'd reconsidered her suggestion.

She seemed glad that I had "relented" and suggested that I ask Pop if he still needed someone to help out down at the mill.

I made my offer at the supper table.

"Why would you want to work at the mill?" Pop wondered. (Apparently Mom hadn't discussed her plan with him before proposing it to me.) "You're a young *lady*, Eleanor, not an office girl!"

"But Pop! Foerster's Mill has been in the family for generations. It's a family treasure! I'd like to know more about how it operates. And maybe I could pick up some skills while I'm there—skills that would be useful later on . . . say, managing a household."

Mom brightened. "There's merit in what Eleanor says, dear. Do you remember how hard it was for *me* to master the art of the household budget?"

Pop chuckled indulgently. "It's not entirely clear to me that you have done so even yet, Lily."

Mom must have talked with him in private over the next few days. On Saturday afternoon, just before dinner, he called me into the parlor for a private meeting. He sat erectly—more so than usual. I had the feeling that this was a formal business meeting, not just a father-daughter conversation, so I sat up straight in my chair as well.

"I have been talking with the office girls: Miss Jennings, my bookkeeper—who will be leaving soon—and Mrs. Brady, who manages files and correspondence. They say that they would welcome a hardworking assistant and would be willing to train her. If you are prepared to keep your nose to the grindstone and follow their instructions, you may join them in the office each week on Thursday and Friday after school and on Saturday morning. If all goes well, you can take Miss Jennings's place when she leaves."

"Oh! Yes!" I cried, forgetting for a moment my businesslike

demeanor. Then, I calmly went on. "If it works out well, might I expect to increase my hours after graduation?"

"We'll see, Eleanor. It depends on you and the girls."

I wouldn't be earning much, but if all went well, I would be able to buy my round-trip ticket before too many months passed by.

My first big job at the mill was mailing the invoices to Pop's clients. I was somewhat apprehensive because this was the very job that had led to Pop's scolding Francis, and perhaps to Francis's quitting and running off to join the army—it seemed like a million years ago. But I managed to handle the task without incident, earning the approval of Miss Jennings and Mrs. Brady—and Pop. I wonder if they gave me that job at the very outset as a test. At any rate, I passed it, and I guessed that meant I could work there as long as I needed to.

My other big moneymaking scheme was to sell a lot more postcard photographs to Mr. Lloyd. I undertook a project to photograph notable buildings all over town, most of which had never been seen as worthy of postcards before now. I took pictures of the school, the churches, Pop's mill, the American Hotel, the library, the courthouse, Johnnie's store, and a bunch of other local landmarks, including handsome old houses like our own. I set out to persuade him that photographs like these would boost the town in general, and some of the businesses would pay to have their own buildings represented. Mr. Lloyd bought the lot; he also continued to send me referrals for new photographs that businesses could use to sell their wares.

Meanwhile, John seemed to be settling into his new home in Oakland. He'd found a studio that he could rent part-time from another photographer—a woman, Irene Fletcher.

Miss Fletcher is a remarkable photographer, he wrote. *Her pictures look as though they come from another world. Indeed, they do—from a world that exists only in her head! She takes photos, all right, but then she blends several of them together into a single image that looks eerie even before she lays a smoky aura on it in the darkroom. She doesn't think of herself as a simple recorder of reality, but as an artist—like a painter. I'm learning a lot from her.*

Indeed, she is giving me my first big chance as a photographer out here in the West. A magazine called Sunset *is planning a story about her and her work. She wants me to take the portrait of her that will appear in the article. In the process, she'll show me how she works her magic on a simple image to turn it into art.*

The magazine came out in April; John was so proud of it that he sent us a dozen copies—one of which I appropriated for myself. John's photograph shows a woman about Mom's age, one who looks strong and athletic, as if she spends much of her time climbing the mountains where many of her own photographs have been taken. Her pictures are haunting, as if from a dream: women in flowing drapery posed against—and sometimes in—blasted mountain trees that seem to have survived in the wilderness for millennia. I pored over the article endlessly, wondering how I might reproduce the magical effects that Miss Fletcher—and now John, I suppose—had achieved. I planned to play with these ideas in the darkroom that John had left for me in the barn.

I decided to take a series of pictures with the idea of blending two or three of them together into one image. Vivian, elfin little creature that she is, would be a perfect character to put into some magical scene. So I set out to take a whole roll of film showing her at play. Maybe one or two of the images would blend with other photographic scenes.

I could see why Miss Fletcher put a smoky haze over her photographs: The "joints" between the images looked pretty clumsy without a bit of camouflage. Ultimately, I came up with some blended photographs that were fairly amusing, if not artful. Vivian was especially taken with the one that shows her twirling like a ballerina at the top of the church steeple.

"Look what *I* did!" she cried to anyone who would listen. Mom worried that one of these days, Vivian might try duplicating her amazing feat on the steeple. Perhaps Mom was right. It might have been wiser to choose a more mature model, one who had already learned the difference between art and real life.

I sent that photograph to John, along with Vivian's reaction. I knew he'd enjoy it!

42

It was May. The last of the snow was long gone, and the crab apple tree in the yard was covered with soft pink blossoms. Lucy and Vivian started taking daily walks together up Verona Street to visit the cemetery. Lucy told me it was a great comfort to pay her respects to Will. Soon, I noticed that Doc sometimes left his office early to join them. On the days when he did, all three of them looked calmer and happier when they arrived home.

Soon thereafter, Lucy invited me into her room for a sisters-only moment. "I wanted to talk with you in private, Ellie," she said. "Something has come up, and I don't know how to respond. I'm hoping that you can help me figure out the right thing to do."

Me? I wondered why she didn't ask Ida—or Mom.

"It's delicate. Today, as the two of us were walking up the street, Vivian called me *Mommy*."

"That's sweet, Lucy, but how is it delicate?"

"I almost cried on the spot—from the thought that her *real* mother, lovely Cora, has already faded from her memory. And I have to admit—though I'm ashamed to say so—that I felt *proud* to see that she cares for me as if I *were* her own mother. Does that make me disloyal to Cora? As much as I dote on the little imp, I never *meant* to turn into Vivian's mother!"

I slipped an arm around Lucy's shoulder—as if *I* were the big sister. "Cora was devoted to Vivian. She would be happy to see her precious baby in such loving care as yours."

"Should I tell her not to call me Mommy any longer?"

"I don't know, Lucy. Maybe you should ask Doc's advice. He's her father, after all."

"I'd *never* ask him! He might think I was *flirting* with him, hinting at taking Cora's place in the family. And both of us widowed for just a few months! Wicked!" With that, she commenced to cry.

I held her in my arms without saying anything. What was there to say?

After that, I watched more closely when the three of them were together. Occasional walks with Vivian became daily walks and seemed to grow longer over time. Lucy and Doc looked happier than I'd seen either one of them since the start of the epidemic.

One night after dinner, Doc and Pop retired to the parlor together. In passing, I wondered if this meant that an engagement—*another* engagement—was afoot. But no. On their return, Pop announced that Doc had entered into a contract to buy John's old place. John would be glad to hear that. He had told us he could use some cash to get himself settled in California.

"It's a lovely old house," Doc observed. "On the small side, but with a fine, big yard for Vivian to play in. It will be easy to turn John's studio into my office. And if we need more living space, there's plenty of room on the lot to expand."

I was glad he'd made the decision to buy John's house. It would have been hard to see it fall into a stranger's hands. I still had one question, though. "What made you decide to move, Doc? You already have a perfectly good home and office right down the street."

Mom sent me a pained look, as if I were prying into things I had no business knowing—much less asking about. But Doc didn't seem reluctant to answer.

"To tell you the truth, Eleanor, I can't imagine moving back there again. The place feels haunted—haunted by my memories of Cora. That's one reason I'm still taking advantage of your family's hospitality to stay here. But it's getting to be time for me to lead my *own* life once more, in my own home."

Lucy was silent during this conversation. But later, after we'd both gone to bed, she crept into my room and woke me as she slipped under the covers. She was crying, again.

"Will's gone. Cora's gone," she sobbed. "It's been but a few months! And here I am, already daydreaming about a future with Doc—before either one of us is out of mourning!" More sobs. "How could I be so selfish? What would people think? What would *Doc* think if he knew?"

I wondered if he'd been thinking along the same lines. But I couldn't say so, not yet. I held her and told her I loved her until she finally sobbed out all her tears and fell asleep.

After that night, I noticed that Lucy and Vivian kept up their habit of walking together every afternoon—but never on their old route, and never with Doc. Sometimes they went past Johnnie's and the other shops on Iroquois, and sometimes they walked along Iroquois in the other direction. I noticed that Vivian fussed a bit about the change at first, but she got used to the new routine.

Evidently Doc did too. Soon I began to notice that whichever way Lucy and Vivian walked, Doc was with them when they returned.

One day in June, Lucy and Doc made the announcement I had been expecting—they announced their engagement at the dinner table.

"Vivian chose her own new mommy," he told us. "She chose well. No one in the world is as kind and loving as is dear Lucy. Both Lucy and I have survived terrible losses in the past year. Both of us have found life again—with each other. We may well face the disapproval of people who think we acted too soon."

"*We* know we haven't," said Lucy. "Vivian is too young to go on for long without a 'real' mommy. And we, all three of us, love one another. Ours will be a marriage of three."

My graduation was only a few weeks away. Lucy and Doc had already decided to wait until after my big day to announce their plans to the world at large. Lucy wanted me as her maid of honor, and Doc hoped that Francis would be home in time to stand up for him.

There was one more complication: Doc's new house was far from ready to move into with his new bride, and he'd already rented his old place to a young dentist who had just moved to town. Doc was fixing up the living quarters for the new tenant, though he would need to continue working out of his old office until his new one, in John's former studio, was ready.

Meanwhile, he and Lucy and Vivian were spending a lot of time at the new house—picking out wallpaper and paint, checking the workmen's daily progress, figuring out what furniture they needed and where it might go.

Their frequent visits seem to have set a few tongues wagging. Mom said that old Mrs. Schultz, who lives next door to Doc's new house, had stopped her on the street to ask what was going on between Lucy and "that young Doctor Baker."

"Why, *nothing*!" said Mom in apparent shock. "I believe your imagination is running away with you! Lucy has been tending to little Vivian ever since she lost her mother. Doc wishes to introduce his child to her new home so as to speed up her adjustment to the change. It stands to reason that Vivian's nursemaid should accompany her on these visits."

According to Mom, Mrs. Schultz looked disappointed, but mollified, and Mom breathed a sigh of relief. "The busybodies in town are going to be shocked *anyway* when they learn that Lucy and Doc are engaged so soon after they lost their loved ones. We don't want them to warm up on their gossip too far in advance!"

43

My grades slipped a bit toward the end of the school year. Billy Warner, the minister's son, inched ahead of me in the final term and became class valedictorian. I think it was the distraction of my photography project—and the fun—that took my mind off school. That and the pleasure of earning my own money.

Mom and Pop were surprisingly calm about it. "Don't worry, dear," said Mom. "You don't need the best grades as much as Billy does. After all, he will be going to college in the fall!"

College. I wondered if I might do that, too, even though I didn't get to be valedictorian. But Mom and Pop had never once brought up the idea of college for me, only for Francis.

"Besides," Mom went on, "young men never like to be outshone by girls. It gets in the way of proper courtship and marriage."

Courtship and marriage didn't have much appeal for me these days. I thought about Rosie and Harold. They had courted themselves straight into a dead end as tenants down on Welk's farm with a baby they were not ready for.

Lucy *was* ready, though. She'd be happy as a wife and mother, I knew.

One day, I may want to get married and have a family, too, but not before I know what I can do on my own. Somehow Mom doesn't see that I take after her. She had to try her wings, too, when she was a girl, first by leaving Yankee Hill to study here in Foersterville, and then by going off to study music in New York City. Both of those moves must have taken some courage for a poor girl from out in the countryside. Going to the big city, and all alone too! I don't believe that I could muster the courage to do what she did.

Visiting John in Oakland would be easier, I thought—even though it's thousands of miles farther away. After arriving there on the train, I wouldn't have to make my own way entirely, as Mom had in New York. After all, John was already settled in Oakland, in his own little bungalow. He had told me he could put me up for a while, and he wanted to show me the sights and introduce me to his new friends. He hadn't mentioned colleges around Oakland, but someday I'd have to ask him about it. Maybe not just yet, but soon . . .

I would have raised the idea of my California visit with the family by now, but I still had some knotty details to work out. If I knew Mom, she'd never let me take a train all the way across the country without a chaperone or an escort, and I couldn't think of anyone she would approve of who would be willing or able to go with me.

Lucy, of course, was too wrapped up with Doc and Vivian, her wedding, and settling into the new house.

Mom was even busier than usual since she was now the only garden club member willing to maintain the Victory Arch over Iroquois Avenue. The other members had lost interest as the war ended and their own people returned. But Mom was determined to keep the decorations looking fresh until Francis finally came home. And there was no telling when that would be.

As always, Pop had his mill to run.

Ida would have been a wonderful travelling companion when she was younger, but she no longer had the stamina she once had. I'd noticed that even walking up to church was getting to be a chore for her these days.

Reid would be excellent company, too, but of course he's the very kind of person Mom thinks I need protection from.

I was about to give up on the whole idea of going west when John's telegram arrived. He was coming for a visit!

And soon! Next Thursday—just two days before my graduation! He must have been planning to go back to California before too long; after all, he'd said in the telegram that he would be coming for a *visit*. Maybe he'd want company when he returned home . . . to California.

John would need a place to stay while he was here in Foersterville. Our own house was filled up, what with Doc still sleeping in Francis's room. Doc couldn't move down to his new place just yet because he and Lucy both thought—and the rest of us agreed—that for the sake of family stability, little Vivian needed to spend every night under the same roof as her daddy. So Doc would continue to stay with us, and he agreed that John could sleep at his old studio down the street. John would even get to use his own shabby old rope bed, one of the few pieces of his furniture Pop hadn't been able to sell or give away.

Lucy and I would go over on Sunday with linens to make up John's bed. I'd already written a note to slip under his pillow in case I didn't have a chance to speak to him in private right away:

Dear John,

Ever since you went away, I've been working hard to earn enough money to visit you in California. Now I have enough to get me there and back, plus a little more to pay for room and board while I'm there. Will you let me come along when you head back?

Your loving niece, Eleanor

PS—I haven't figured out how to raise the subject with Mom and Pop. If you're willing, can you help me work out a plan that they might agree to?

I hoped John liked my idea. I didn't know what I'd do if he turned me down.

Late Sunday night—or was it early Monday morning?—I heard a noise downstairs. Was it the front door? Then the quiet squeaking of floorboards, something that sounded like a grunt or a growl. I was too sleepy to bestir myself or even to think clearly—and maybe a little frightened as well. Was it a dream? Or John, home earlier than he'd expected? A burglar? I'd know when I woke up the next day, I told myself, and promptly fell asleep again.

Everything seemed normal in the morning. We all had a quiet breakfast around the kitchen table. Then it was time for Pop and me to head off to the mill for a day "at the old grindstone," as Pop was fond of saying.

As we gathered our coats and hats in the front hall, a deep roar came out of the parlor next to us: "*Who* the *hell* has taken over *my* bedroom!" A bearded man, filthy and bedraggled in what I thought at first were khaki work clothes, came charging out of the parlor toward us.

I recognized him through my panic. "Francis!"

Mom raced from the kitchen. "My dear boy! Are you home? Oh, how I wish I'd known you were coming today! I'd have prepared such a welcome for you!" She reached out to embrace him, but he pulled away.

"So much for my goddamn surprise homecoming." His voice dripped with sarcasm as he bowed melodramatically toward Mom. "*Please* accept my *profound* apologies that my return was a *disappointment* to you. You think it's a disappointment for *you*? Look at *me*! I get home in the middle of the night and find some clown sleeping in my bed. Then my own mother is upset that she didn't have a chance to turn my homecoming into a goddamn party!" He clenched his fists.

"And last night at the bar, I find out that Bess Welk went off and married some idiot farmer down by Binghamton who is too dumb to count up to nine. He thinks *my* goddamn daughter is *his*!"

Then Francis looked at me for the first time. "Sorry, little sister. I shouldn't have exposed you to this . . . stuff. Why don't you head off for school now?"

"School's over. I'm working down at the mill with Pop."

"So you're in on it, *too*, then. You took over *my* job. I never thought my favorite sister would betray me, along with everybody else."

He stomped out of the house and disappeared down Iroquois Avenue.

Pop and I both cried all the way to the mill. I've never seen him cry like that.

That was the last we saw of Francis for days.

It was John who finally spotted him. John had eaten supper with us on his first night back in town. After supper he was heading down Iroquois on the way to his old house when he saw Francis coming down the front steps of the American Hotel. Francis looked as though he'd been drinking. A lot. He never saw John, who followed him to the back of the hotel and saw him stumble through a basement door into the seediest room in the whole place, right next to the coal cellar. It was probably the noisiest room too. The railroad tracks weren't more than twenty feet away. John was tired after his long trip and decided not to try to talk with Francis that night. He decided he'd come by in the morning, when they'd both be able to think better after a night's sleep.

The wait may have been a mistake. The next morning, John knocked on Francis's door. No answer. The door turned out to be unlocked, so John opened it and stepped inside. It took him a few minutes to see that nobody was there. There were filthy clothes, bottles, and food scraps all over the floor and the unmade bed. The place stank. When John's foot brushed against a grease-stained paper sack on the floor, out dashed a big rat that went scurrying off to safety under the bed. That was enough for John. He made a quick exit.

"I've seen many a hobo camp along the tracks from here to California and back," he told us over breakfast. "Even hoboes take better care of their camps than that! Good old Francis always had his weaknesses, but hobnobbing with *rats* has never been one of them."

For as long as he had been staying with us, Doc had always avoided commenting on our family matters, but now he made an exception. He said, "Francis is not alone in his despair. Recently I've seen a few other veterans who seem haunted, like Francis—by what he saw in battle, perhaps, or by what he did in battle, or failed to do, or by what he learned about himself in the process. I could be mistaken, but I believe he was raging inside even before he got here—hoping for a soothing return to an unchanged Foersterville, but shoving away the very people who want to offer him comfort. We need to believe in his capacity to grow beyond the horror and disappointment he has experienced. Our love and understanding can go a long way toward helping Francis recover."

Love and understanding. But I was scared. How could I give love and understanding to someone who scared me to death?

44

After all the excitement (and horror) of the previous few days, graduation on Friday was quite a letdown. We girls all wore pretty white dresses, and the boys wore ties and suits with long trousers. Mr. Silas handed out the diplomas very . . . very . . . deliberately . . . in a process that made me glad we had one of the smaller classes in recent years. Billy also gave his valedictory address, which seemed to me as if it had been copied straight from one of his father's duller sermons. I scanned the audience for Francis. I knew everyone else was there: Mom and Pop, Ida, Lucy, Doc, little Vivian (on her best behavior), John, Reid, Mr. Lloyd the stationer, Johnnie the grocer, and even my old friend Rosie, holding her baby in her arms.

Only my brother was missing. It was a disappointment, a *big* disappointment, but not a surprise. Pop had talked with the hotel owner, who told him that Francis had just started a job that would take him out of town, sometimes for several days at a time. He was working for the railroad, checking up and down the line for damage to the tracks. He traveled alone in a handcar, sometimes pulling off onto a siding to rest. Maybe that lonely life was what he needs right now.

At dinner after the graduation ceremony, John picked up on my idea of going out West with him—even before we'd had a chance to hatch our plan together. It took me a minute to realize his proposal was even grander than my own.

"Ellie is such a good photographer already that my California friends who have seen her work want to meet her and take her under their wing. I have to admit that she's already as good an artist as I am, and I think she has it in her to be an even better one. I want her to come with me back to California. It will be good for her future—and mine too."

Mom looked skeptical.

"Ask Mr. Lloyd," John continued. "He told me this morning that Ellie is the best young photographer he's ever seen. He's been working all this year to give a boost to her career."

He looked seriously at Mom. "Lily, Eleanor is like you—and like me too. She has a talent that has to bloom away from home. You and I need to support that gift, just as our parents supported yours—and you supported mine."

"But California is so far away! What if it doesn't go well?"

"Remember, Lily, I'll be there with her. I can help her pick up the pieces if she has to. My bet, though, is that she'll fly through it all—and love the challenge."

Pop looked pensive. "If Eleanor goes to California, there will be space at the mill for Francis to return to his old job. I'm not confident that that would be good for the mill, but . . ."

"Come to think of it, you have a good point, Arthur," Mom added. "It might help to bring Francis back into the fold."

Then she turned to me. "What do you think, dear?"

She *asked* me!

"Francis needs to come home."

And I needed to leave—but not before my big sister's big day.

Lucy and Doc married in our backyard a few days after graduation. John filled in as best man because Francis was still missing—and Lucy and Doc couldn't have counted on his being available even if they had been able to find him. I was the maid of honor. Vivian, of course, loved being the flower girl. She ate a fair percentage of her flowers.

The three of them took off in Doc's automobile for a brief honeymoon together, giving John a chance to stay with us—and *them* a chance to move into their new home when they returned. John helped carry Lucy's canopy bed down the street and brought his old rope bed to our house to take its place.

If Francis comes home, his own room is ready for him. So is his job at the mill. Maybe Union College will accept him—if he decides he wants to go there. Or maybe he'll find his own future when he heals enough to imagine it.

John and I spent most of Saturday out in the stable, sorting through his store of photographic equipment for the things he'd need in his new studio in California. We filled up two big old steamer trunks that Pop had pulled out of some forgotten nook in the hayloft. Then we sat on the trunks to force them shut and buckled each one fast with a couple of broad leather straps. Finally, John glued on sturdy tags with his name and his new address.

"The only problem we have now is getting these behemoths down to the station," said John with a heavy sigh.

"That's no difficulty on *this* end, John. I have the solution right . . . here!" I stepped into the other stall, the one with all of Reid's books, and pulled out his beat-up old wheelbarrow. It was just big enough to roll one trunk at a time down to the station before we gathered for supper back at our house.

On our way back from the second trip, we ran into Reid himself.

"What have we *here*?" he asked melodramatically. "Two suspicious characters making off with my wheeled vehicle!"

"Yes," John replied. "We're taking it to our hideout in Foerster's barn. Would you care for a ride?"

Reid folded himself into the wheelbarrow and John and I hauled him up the hill to the barn, hitting every rut and bump we could find along the way. Once we were in our barn hideout, we all turned serious.

Reid said, "I've been wanting to talk with you, John, before you go back to California—to thank you. I would not have been able to get an education without your help. You housed me and hired me and gave me inspiration. I've never thanked you for that, and it's well past time I did." He smiled in that Mephistophelian way of his. "*You're* the one who deserves a ride in the wheelbarrow!"

I piped in. "John is doing the same for me. He convinced Mom and Pop to let me go to California with him. Tomorrow. For an education."

"Not you too, Ellie! But if all my favorite people are going out to California, maybe I should too. Someday. They say that radio stations will be going up all over the country soon. Maybe in California!"

The next day, Sunday, John and I left. The family gathered at the station to bid us goodbye. Reid was there too. I knew I'd miss them all.

Just as we were getting underway, a handcar came slogging up the tracks from behind us. A handsome, *shaven* man was pumping it. Francis!

We called out to each other at the same moment, it seemed: "Remember! I *love* you!"

And we were on our way.

A Note on Francis's Letters

E*llie's Great War* includes letters from Francis Foerster to his family back home. Most of their content is my own creation, but letters that deal with battlefield conditions in France contain direct quotes from contemporary soldiers to their own families. Willard Dann, my father's cousin, is the source of most of these passages; others come from soldiers whose letters were published in hometown newspapers during 1918.

All of these men served honorably. None was a model for Francis's weaknesses.

Acknowledgments

I owe a great debt to a band of muses whose enthusiastic support helped me through the rough parts of creating *Ellie's Great War*:

The Lake Park Writers' Group, whose creativity inspired my own

Lee Weisenfelder, a vivid writer and a great sport, who sat through two full oral readings of my book, offering helpful comments along the way

John Coll, who introduced me to the life and work of the pioneering California photographer Anne Brigman, on whom I based my character Irene Fletcher

Suzy Spradlin, who gave me insight into one of the utopian artists' and writers' havens of the early twentieth century

Maria Cheng, who arranged my first public reading from *Ellie's Great War*

Corinne Beauvais, who shared with me the World War I diary of her father, Octave P. Beauvais, an ambulance driver in France

Peter Lindemann, a historian of Schoharie County, New York, whose work on that community's involvement in World War I was helpful background for my own effort

Carolee Inskeep, the most enthusiastic genealogist in our family.

About the Author

photo credit: Anne Keech

Diane Keech is a native of upstate New York, the setting of *Ellie's Great War.* She has lived on the West Coast for most of her adult life. While doing research for another writing project, she came across a trove of letters that boys from her hometown had sent from the front during World War I. Those letters sparked her curiosity about the effects of the Great War and its aftermath on the families left behind. *Ellie's Great War,* her first novel, grew from that spark.

Looking for your next great read?

We can help!

Visit www.shewritespress.com/next-read or scan the QR code below for a list of our recommended titles.

She Writes Press is an award-winning independent publishing company founded to serve women writers everywhere.